He liked playing

"You've got some swelling in your ankles," he said, lifting her legs onto the bedcovers.

His large yet tender hands on her skin had Elizabeth struggling to remember which of them was the real doctor. "That's normal," she croaked, "considering I'm six weeks away from having a baby."

Matt was persistent. "Want a foot massage? How about a back rub?"

Just the thought of his hands touching her all over her body had her pulse racing. What was wrong with her? She was almost eight months pregnant and getting hot and bothered by a stubborn cowboy who didn't know how to take no for an answer. Instantly, she pulled the quilt over her legs.

"Well, in that case, I'll be on my way." He made for the door, but not before he shot her a smile that traveled all the way to his eyes. "Sleep tight, Elizabeth."

Dear Reader,

As the hectic holiday season begins, take a moment to treat yourself to a fantastic love story from Harlequin American Romance. All four of our wonderful books this month are sure to please your every reading fancy.

Beloved author Cathy Gillen Thacker presents us with *A Cowboy Kind of Daddy*, the fourth and final title in her series THE McCABES OF TEXAS. Travis McCabe is the last eligible bachelor in the family and you know his matchmaking parents are not about to let him miss heading to the altar.

Also wrapping up this month is our special series DELIVERY ROOM DADS. Judy Christenberry's memorable *Baby 2000* has a truly heroic McIntyre brother caring for an expectant mother who just may have the first baby of the millennium.

Two holiday stories finish up the month with tales that will bring you lots of seasonal joy. Pamela Bauer pens a delightful small-town romance with *Saving Christmas*, and Jacqueline Diamond brings us an emotional story of unexpected reunions with *Mistletoe Daddy*.

Here's hoping your holiday season is filled with happiness, good health—and lots of romance!

Melissa Jeglinski
Associate Senior Editor

Baby 2000

JUDY CHRISTENBERRY

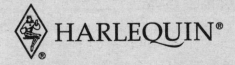

HARLEQUIN®

TORONTO • NEW YORK • LONDON
AMSTERDAM • PARIS • SYDNEY • HAMBURG
STOCKHOLM • ATHENS • TOKYO • MILAN • MADRID
PRAGUE • WARSAW • BUDAPEST • AUCKLAND

ISBN 0-373-16802-0

BABY 2000

Copyright © 1999 by Judy Christenberry.

Printed in U.S.A.

ABOUT THE AUTHOR

Judy Christenberry has been writing romances for fifteen years because she loves happy endings as much as her readers. Judy quit teaching French recently and devoted her time to writing. She hopes readers have as much fun reading her stories as she does writing them. She spends her spare time reading, watching her favorite sports teams and keeping track of her two daughters. Judy's a native Texan, living in Plano, a suburb of Dallas.

Books by Judy Christenberry

HARLEQUIN AMERICAN ROMANCE

555—FINDING DADDY
570   WHO'S THE DADDY?
612—WANTED. CHRISTMAS MOMMY
626—DADDY ON DEMAND
649—COWBOY CUPID*
653—COWBOY DADDY*
661—COWBOY GROOM*
665—COWBOY SURRENDER*
701—IN PAPA BEAR'S BED
726—A COWBOY AT HEART
735—MY DADDY THE DUKE
744—COWBOY COME HOME*
755—COWBOY SANTA
773—ONE HOT DADDY-TO-BE?**
777—SURPRISE–YOU'RE A DADDY!**
781—DADDY UNKNOWN**
785—THE LAST STUBBORN COWBOY**
802—BABY 2000

*   4 Brides for 4 Brothers
** 4 Tots for 4 Texans

And watch for Judy's next Harlequin American Romance novel,
THE GREAT TEXAS WEDDING BARGAIN, available in March 2000.

Dear Reader,

When our editors asked us to write stories about three brothers who wind up in the delivery room near midnight, December 31, 1999, we sat down to think. Good-looking men, pregnant ladies with brains and beauty, and a first-baby-of-the-millennium contest—how could we resist?

The friendship we formed as we created DELIVERY ROOM DADS was an added bonus. E-mails flew fast and furiously, and when the dust settled, we had a town, a family, a contest and happily-ever-after for everyone involved.

Welcome to Bison City, Wyoming, home of the devastating McIntyre brothers. The baby race begins in Karen Toller Whittenburg's *Baby by Midnight?*, complications arise in Muriel Jensen's *Countdown to Baby* and the winner is revealed at the stroke of midnight in Judy Christenberry's *Baby 2000*. Our characters remind us of the love and strength of family. We hope they do the same for you, too. Thank you for joining us in the delivery room as these special dads ring in the new millennium!

Karen Toller Whittenburg
Muriel Jensen
Judy Christenberry

Chapter One

He was a fraud.

Matt McIntyre sighed as he hurried out of the feed store into the cold winter air. He needed to get back to the ranch and do some work. Hopefully he wouldn't run into any more well-wishers on his way, eager to discuss the baby boom in Bison City, Wyoming.

Bison City wasn't a big town. Everyone knew his neighbor and his neighbor's neighbor. And the feed store was a popular meeting place for the men of the town. So it hadn't been a surprise for him to see his neighbors and friends.

But he hadn't expected them all to be talking about babies. Horses, sure, cows, of course. Even the occasional cattle rustling. But babies? Matt had smiled, shaken hands with everyone in the feed store, it seemed, agreed all the pregnancies were wonderful, especially those in his family.

And hated every minute.

Guilt filled him. It wasn't that he wasn't happy for his brothers and sister. Or the whole damn town, for that matter. But every mention of the babies to come, the new lives that would fill the town and the surrounding ranches reminded him of his own loss.

Julie and their unborn son.

He and Julie had married almost six years ago. They'd wanted children, but, in spite of their best efforts, she hadn't gotten pregnant. Then, after four years of trying, they'd received the good news.

Without thinking, Matt came to a halt, staring into space, remembering the excitement that had lit up Julie's face, the joy that had filled him. Only to be followed by utter despair when her car had slid out of control on an unexpected icy patch of road, taking her directly into the path of an eighteen-wheeler.

They'd tried to save the baby's life, but at six months, the child, injured also, couldn't make it.

He'd buried them both and tried to get on with his life.

He guessed he hadn't done as good a job as he'd thought, because when Josie, his sister, had announced her pregnancy, he'd discovered pain deep within him. Pain that had been festering for two long years.

Then everyone discovered Annie Thatcher's pregnancy. Annie had been Matt's brother Alex's girl for as long as anyone could remember.

Annie never said the baby was Alex's. But when he'd come home in October, it seemed he believed he was the daddy.

Someone bumped into Matt, and he smiled in

apology and moved on. That was another area where he needed to improve. Matt had tried to advise Alex. He'd tried to help Alex. He'd tried— He'd driven Alex away.

Damn, he should've kept his mouth shut. Instead he'd taken his big-brother role too seriously.

"Watch out!" someone yelled.

Matt looked up in time to see a woman crossing the street, her back to him, and a car coming too fast. Was that Bailey? His heart pumping, Matt dashed forward and grabbed an arm, yanking the woman out of harm's way. He fell to the snowy sidewalk, her body on top of his.

As he clasped her to him, he felt the rounded tummy of an expectant mom.

"Damn it, Bailey, you've got to be more careful!" he exclaimed as he sat up. Bailey was his middle brother's lady, also pregnant. It was definitely an epidemic.

It wasn't Bailey. The blonde, her hair tucked up under a knit cap, turned to look at him, her cheeks pale.

"I'm not Bailey, but you're right, I do need to be more careful. Sorry, I had a lot on my mind." Her voice was low, soothing, but he heard the tremors in it.

She was sitting on his lap and he still had his arms wrapped around her pregnant stomach. When he felt a jab, his eyes widened and he jerked his hands back.

"Sorry again, I think my daughter is protesting." Her smile warmed as she recovered from the shock.

"You're having a girl?"

She nodded. Then she tried to scoot off his lap.

"Getting up may take a while unless someone comes along to assist," she said, a rueful smile on her face.

Matt spotted a friend hurrying toward them. "Hey, Jack, come give us a hand."

"I'm comin'," Jack Dubois, his neighbor, assured him. "I saw you save Dr. Elizabeth. I wasn't close enough. How are you, Doc?"

Matt stared at the woman sitting on top of him. This was the new OB-GYN who'd come to town recently, the one who had the job of delivering all the babies?

"How are you going to deliver the babies when you're having one yourself?" he asked abruptly.

After shooting him a puzzled look, she extended her hands to his neighbor. "I appreciate the help, Mr. Dubois," she said. To Matt, she added, "Being pregnant doesn't render me useless."

Matt scrambled to his feet as soon as she was upright, but he didn't let her leave. "Where are you going?"

She blinked several times, and he noticed her hazel eyes, flecks of gold and green touched with brown. "Home. Thank you again for your assistance. And you, too, Mr. Dubois."

Jack touched his hat and excused himself. Matt said goodbye to his friend, but he took hold of the doctor's arm. "Where's home?"

"I have a house over on Astor Drive near the

hospital. Why? Were you thinking of visiting me?''
She lifted one eyebrow and smiled.

Though he knew teasing when he heard it—after
all, he had two brothers and a sister—he took her
seriously. ''I'm *thinking* of taking you home. You
should rest after such a stressful event.''

''That's all right. The walking will be good for
me.'' She turned to leave, but he held on.

''Sorry, lady. You can walk another time. I'm
taking you home.''

ELIZABETH LEE couldn't hold back a smile. The
man certainly lived up to the image he presented.
Macho cowboy. Take-charge kind of guy.

But he had no business taking charge of her.

She didn't even know him, though he did look
familiar. ''I appreciate your concern, but I don't
even know who you are. And I don't need you to
make decisions for me.''

''I'm Matt McIntyre, Josie's oldest brother.''

Well, that explained why he looked familiar.
She'd already met both Jeff and Alex. It seemed
the genes ran true in the McIntyre family. ''I'm
pleased to meet you, Mr. McIntyre. And again, I
appreciate your rescuing me. Now, if you'll excuse
me,'' she continued, assuming he would release her.

He didn't.

''Lady, do you know how many women in this
town are counting on you to bring their babies into
this world?''

She laughed. ''Yes, Mr. McIntyre, I believe I do.

You see, they are my patients and we keep records of these things.''

He smiled in return and she felt her heart flutter. The man was certainly attractive, even when frowning, but when he smiled, he made the sun seem pale in comparison. How silly of her to react, she admonished herself. She wasn't interested in any man, no matter what her patients thought.

He began pulling her toward a large truck.

''Mr. McIntyre, unhand me!''

''No, ma'am. It's my duty to get you safely home.''

She couldn't believe this man. What was wrong with him? Didn't he understand the word *no?* Elizabeth was a patient woman, but she was about to lose her temper. When she saw a police car coming down the street, she figured she could solve her problem without that happening.

Waving frantically, she was relieved when the car pulled to a stop beside the two of them and the driver rolled down his window.

''Howdy, ma'am, Matt. Everything all right?'' The policeman didn't seem alarmed.

''This man is kidnapping me!'' Elizabeth blurted.

The cowboy beside her chuckled and shook his head. ''The lady was almost hit by a truck and fell. In her condition, she should go home and put her feet up. I'm trying to make sure she gets there, but she thinks she should walk.''

The deputy smiled at the man beside her. ''Good job, Matt,'' he said before he turned to her. ''I can assure you, Dr. Lee, that Matt is perfectly safe.

He'll take good care of you. Have a nice day, now.''

And he drove off.

''Have a nice—'' Elizabeth sputtered, unable to believe what had just happened. The people of Bison City had warmly welcomed her, willing to do anything to help her settle in. But when she complained of being kidnapped, the police said, ''Have a nice day''?

That definitely wouldn't do.

''I thought that was right neighborly of him,'' Matt McIntyre said, using that devastating smile again. ''Do you need me to carry you, or do you want to walk to my truck?''

''Carry me? You lay one hand on me—'' She broke off to stare at his big hand clasped around her arm. ''I mean, another hand on me, and I'll scream bloody murder!''

He seemed to find her threat humorous.

Okay, so she knew he wasn't kidnapping her. And maybe she was overreacting, but no meant no. Except to Matt McIntyre. She remembered her refusal to become involved in the Bison City baby contest for the first baby born in the new millennium. Must be a family thing, because Josie McIntyre Moore, the coordinator, had definitely ignored that no, too.

Before she'd finished that thought, she discovered herself at the passenger side of the big truck she'd noticed. Matt opened the door, then turned to put his hands around her swollen middle.

"What are you doing?" she demanded, her pulse racing.

"Helping you into the truck," he explained, as if she were a child. "You're a little thing and—"

"I am not little! I'm five foot five. That's average height for a woman."

"Honey, out West, we grow them a little bigger. Josie's got a couple of inches on you. Put your foot on the floorboard," he ordered, then boosted her up.

She landed on the seat with a thump that wasn't much better than her earlier unplanned landing. Turning to protest, she found herself looking out the glass. Matt had already shut the door and was walking around the front of the truck.

The man was impossible.

After getting in, he started the truck and backed it out into the street, seemingly unaffected by the snow that covered everything.

The snow was the reason she'd walked to the store. She still hadn't learned to drive on it well. "Doesn't the snow bother you?"

He stared at her. "Why would it?"

"It's slick."

A shadow seemed to cross his face. Then he shrugged and turned his attention to the driving. "Yeah. But my truck's heavy and I have snow tires. Ice is much more dangerous."

She had nothing to add to that statement. Besides, she'd forgotten she was supposed to be angry with him. She crossed her arms over her stomach and stared straight ahead.

"Tell me which house is yours," he ordered as he turned onto her street.

She was tempted to refuse to direct him. That would show him he couldn't order her around. But it would also prolong their togetherness. "The third one on the right."

As he stopped the truck, she grabbed the door handle, eager to put some distance between her and Matt McIntyre.

"Wait!" he ordered, killing the motor and jumping out of the truck.

Surprised, she was distracted from her intentions. When she realized what he was doing, however, she hurriedly opened her door and began the task of getting down from the high seat. Just as she was sliding off the seat, big hands lifted her down.

With a frustrated huff she muttered, "Thanks." Then she circled him and started up the walk. She heard the door close behind her with satisfaction. Now he'd circle the truck and get in and drive off. Thank goodness!

"Your keys?" a deep voice demanded, and a hand came in front of her. He hadn't left.

"Yes, I have them," she assured him, continuing to carefully negotiate the snow-covered sidewalk.

"Yeah, but what I meant was give them to me."

He'd done it again. Surprised her into turning into a statue. She stared at him, her mouth open in surprise. "Why would I do that?"

"So I can open the door for you."

She started walking again. "You think I'm incapable of opening my own door?"

"Look, I can have the door open and come back and get you before you can get there. This snow is dangerous."

She stopped again, putting her hands on her non-existent waist. "Do you see those tracks leading away from my door? Those are mine. I walked out earlier, and I'll walk in now. I don't need you to carry me."

"Okay."

Which made her even more angry. That was all he was going to say? After all the trouble he'd caused her, he accepted her latest protest with an okay?

And what was wrong with her? She normally didn't let someone upset her. Sarah was going to be furious with her.

She reached the steps and grabbed the wrought-iron rail. Even angry, she had no intention of taking risks. Apparently the man beside her didn't, either. She felt his hand at the small of her back, as if guiding her.

"Go away," she muttered.

"Can't do that," he said with a calm that told her he didn't think she meant those words. "I wouldn't be able to sleep tonight worrying about whether or not you made it safe inside."

"Then you need to get a life. If all you have to worry about is a woman you've never met before, you have way too much time on your hands."

"I may not have met you, but I know all about you," he said. "You're delivering half my family. And you're pregnant, too. And alone."

She reached the porch and dug into the pocket of her jacket. She found her keys just as the thought that they might've fallen out during her fall struck her. With a sigh of relief she inserted the house key in the hole and turned it.

At last she would be free of the persistent baby-sitter.

Turning, she began, "Thank you, I guess, for your help. I'll be fine—"

"I'll just come in and make you a cup of cocoa while you put your feet up."

Without waiting for her approval, he pushed the door back and scooted her out of the way with hands on her shoulders.

A *domesticated* macho cowboy? He wanted to fix her hot chocolate? He thought she should give him free rein in her kitchen while she put her feet up?

A heavenly thought, but she had no intention—

He'd already reached the kitchen. "You don't have any milk."

If she wasn't careful, the next thing she knew, he'd be making a grocery list.

"I finished it this morning," she said without thinking. "I mean, never mind. I'll fix myself some tea later. You can go now. I'm safe inside."

He didn't come out of the kitchen. She hurried over to be sure he did as she said. Instead, he was putting on the teakettle.

"When's your baby due?"

"The eighth of January. You can—"

"Who's the father?"

IF MATT HAD EVER HEARD the doctor was pregnant—maybe Josie had told him—he hadn't listened. Josie talked a lot, and when the subject turned to babies, he usually shut her out.

But he'd definitely heard the doctor was single.

His question seemed to have surprised her.

"I— No one's asked that."

It was his turn to be surprised. "You've been here four months, as pregnant as the rest of the ladies, and no one's asked you how you got that way?"

Her smile surprised him, too. "You know, Mr. McIntyre, I think most everyone understands *how* I got this way."

He smiled back. "Yeah, I guess they do. Especially in Bison City, with half the population pregnant and the other half responsible for it."

"I don't know about half, but there are a lot of babies coming." Her hand was rubbing her stomach in a circle pattern.

"Everything all right?" he asked, his gaze fastened on that small hand.

She jerked her hand down from her stomach. "Yes, of course. I was just assuring Sarah that everything is all right."

"Sarah?"

She blushed, and he squashed an urge to warm his hands against her cheeks. "That's what I named my baby. Sarah Elizabeth."

"Pretty name. Is she jumping around?"

"A little."

"You're sure she's all right?"

She rolled her eyes. "I am the doctor, aren't I? I mean, you didn't suddenly turn in your cowboy hat for a stethoscope, did you?"

His grin widened. "No, ma'am. But I've delivered a few calves, so if you need some help come Christmastime, just let me know."

She pretended to shudder. This cowboy was too much fun. "Thanks, but I believe the ladies would prefer me to do the delivering."

"Actually," he drawled, still smiling, "I'd prefer it, too. Especially when it comes to Josie. She'd light into me if I even thought about delivering her baby."

"Well, I'm glad to know you listen to *some* women," she returned, reminded of her earlier reaction to his bossiness.

Before he could comment, the teakettle began whistling.

"Where's the tea? And a mug?" he asked, turning to the stove.

"I'll take care of it. Really, there's no need—" she began as he opened cabinet doors until he found the cups. Without protesting again, she opened the pantry and took out two teabags, caffeine free.

"You use two teabags?" he asked.

"No, one's for you."

"Uh, I don't usually—"

"You're the one who insisted I have tea. I don't like to drink alone. I've heard it's bad for you."

"Tea's bad for you?" he demanded, urgency in his voice.

She stared at him before gently saying, "I was

teasing. It was the drinking alone I was talking about. Only I think that applies to alcohol, not tea. I was asking you to join me.''

''Oh. Oh, sure. Yeah, I'll drink tea with you.''

The seriousness of his voice reminded her of his earlier protectiveness. Poor man. She could've told him she needed him to paint her house, and he would grab a paintbrush, no questions asked. His wife must— ''Are you married?''

The cup he'd just reached for thudded onto the cabinet. He drew a deep breath before he spoke, and she wondered why that question was so startling.

''No. I'm not married.''

''I didn't mean to pry. The thought occurred to me and— I mean, I know you don't have a *pregnant* wife because she's not on the list of patients, but—''

''No.'' Though his response wasn't loud, she could hear a harshness in his voice that warned her she'd touched a nerve. Was that pain the reason he was so attentive to whatever he thought she needed?

She should drop it. But she couldn't. She'd always been curious. Too curious for her own good. ''You've been married.'' It wasn't a question. She already knew the answer.

He glared at her and shoved the two cups toward her. ''What do we do? Put the teabags in the kettle? Or in the cups?''

''In the cups.''

She handed a teabag to him and unwrapped her

own, setting it in one of the white mugs. He copied her. Since he'd ignored her words, she decided to say nothing else about Matt McIntyre's private life.

He surprised her again. "I've been married. And my wife was pregnant. But she and the baby died."

Then, without another word, the persistent, determined cowboy turned on his heel and strode out of her house.

Chapter Two

Matt cursed himself under his breath. He didn't like leaving a job undone. Particularly because of his weakness. He never talked of Julie or the precious baby boy with anyone, even his family. He sure wasn't going to do so with a stranger.

But the lady needed protecting. She might have a delayed reaction to her fall. He reached into his coat pocket for the cell phone he usually carried.

"Josie? You need to call Dr. Lee."

"Why? What's wrong?" his little sister demanded.

She never changed. Whenever he told her to do something, she always had to know why before she'd agree. With a sigh, he said, "She fell earlier today, and you need to check if she's okay."

"She fell? What happened?"

"She almost got run over crossing the street. I pulled her back, but we fell. I'd just feel better if someone checked on her." He was pleased that his voice sounded so calm, so casual.

"Of course I'll check on her. The Thanksgiving

Fair is tomorrow. She's got to be there. You're coming, aren't you, Matt?''

Damn, he'd been avoiding that topic. Now he'd have to disappoint Josie. ''Uh, no, I can't make it.''

''But, Matt...''

''Let me know when you've checked on the doc.'' Then he turned off his phone. Josie didn't give up on anything important to her, and this damned Millennium Baby Contest was her baby for the moment.

He just couldn't handle being surrounded by pregnant women.

ELIZABETH FINISHED MAKING her cup of tea, but her mind was filled with Matt McIntyre. Not because he was handsome, though, of course, he was. No, she wasn't interested in a man in that way. She was a widow, and she didn't intend to marry again.

She couldn't get him out of her head because he needed help. She knew the limitations of her career. She'd faced those limitations when her husband had died, and she, a doctor, could do nothing to save him.

She'd vowed never to walk away from anyone she could help. And she could help Matt McIntyre. He hadn't dealt with his loss. The pain in his eyes was as fresh as if his wife and child had died yesterday.

The phone interrupted her thoughts.

''Elizabeth?'' Josie responded to her greeting. ''Are you all right?''

''Of course I'm all right. Why wouldn't I be?''

"Well, Matt said—"

"Your brother called you and asked you to check on me." It wasn't a question. She should've been expecting a follow-up. The man was compulsive.

"Yes. He said you fell."

"On him. He's the one who'll have bruises."

"He can handle them. I'm glad you're okay. So, you'll be there tomorrow?"

Elizabeth smiled. "I think that's the only reason you called, Josie Moore. You don't care about me," she teased, "just your contest!"

"You know that's not true. I also called because I learned a long time ago to do what Matt tells me to do. He's bossy!"

"I think I can believe that," Elizabeth agreed, her tone dry.

"Uh-oh, did he boss you around?"

"You could say that. Will he be there tomorrow?" Somehow she wasn't surprised when Josie said no. "Josie, does he ever talk about his wife and baby?"

Silence followed her question. Finally, in a quiet voice, Josie asked, "How do you know about Julie and the baby?"

"He mentioned them, though not by name."

"Matt actually told you about them?" Josie's voice was incredulous.

"Just in passing. He never talks about them?"

"No. He's…he's given a little advice to the guys lately since we're all pregnant, but that's all."

"You know that's not healthy, don't you?" Elizabeth asked. "He needs to open up, talk about it."

Her friend Josie, known for her good humor, grumbled, "You're not telling me something I don't know. I've tried to encourage him to date, but—"

Gently, Elizabeth interrupted, "He can't do that until he's dealt with his past."

"I know. But he's a stubborn cuss."

Elizabeth chuckled. "That's something else you didn't need to tell me." She drew a deep breath. "How long ago did Julie die?"

"Over two years ago. Her car hit a patch of ice and slid into the path of an eighteen-wheeler."

"Oh, my." Just hearing about the accident was upsetting. She couldn't imagine losing someone she loved in such a fashion.

"Elizabeth, is he— I mean, he's going to be okay, isn't he?"

She could hear the love and concern in Josie's voice. "He will be if he deals with his loss. If not, I suspect he'll grow more and more withdrawn."

"We don't want that! We want him to be happy. Matt has always taken care of all of us. We want the best for him. Can you help him, Elizabeth? I've tried, but obviously I'm not doing a good job."

Elizabeth already knew she wanted to help Matt McIntyre, but having Josie's support would make it easier. "Of course. Though it would be better if he saw a psychologist. Is there one in Bison City?"

"No! I mean, no, there's no psychologist, but even if there were, Matt wouldn't be caught dead going to see him."

"Then he probably won't want to see an OB-

GYN, either.'' A mental picture of Matt sitting in her waiting room surrounded by pregnant women teased her sense of the ridiculous.

''Do you have to tell him you're treating him? Can't you just...I don't know, pretend you're interested in him or something?''

Elizabeth gasped and then coughed, almost choking at Josie's words. ''Josie, you can't be serious. I'm seven months pregnant! Matt would run so fast from me you wouldn't see him for a year.''

Silence. Then Josie said in a quiet voice, ''He needs help, Elizabeth. I don't know who to turn to.''

''Would he see Dave?'' Elizabeth asked, naming her partner.

''Matt doesn't go to the doctor at all, unless he breaks something.''

''Ah. Macho man.''

''Yeah. All cowboys are like that.''

''Look,'' Elizabeth began with a sigh, ''I'll do anything I can for your brother, but there may not be much opportunity. You can help if you talk about his wife around him.''

''I'll try,'' Josie agreed, though she didn't sound very sure of herself.

''We both will. And remember, you're not supposed to do a lot of worrying. Happy thoughts for a happy baby.''

''Right. And I'll see you tomorrow at the Thanksgiving Fair.''

''I'll be there.''

WHEN MATT REACHED the ranch, he headed for the kitchen, where he knew Willie, their housekeeper, could be found.

"Did Josie call?"

"Hi, to you, too," Willie returned. "Nope, she hasn't."

Matt frowned. Maybe there was a problem. Maybe the woman had needed help. Damn, he shouldn't have left her. He grabbed the phone and punched in Josie's number.

When he heard her voice, he growled, "You didn't call back."

"I was waiting until this evening. I figured you'd be outside."

"I just got here. Was everything all right?"

"Elizabeth is fine. She said you were bossy."

Matt rolled his eyes, but, of course, Josie couldn't see him. "Sometimes people need to be bossed. She doesn't have anyone to take care of her. What happened to the father of her baby?"

"I don't know."

Matt was shocked. Josie never let anyone keep secrets. "You don't know? Why not? Didn't you ask her?"

"No, I didn't. It's none of my business."

"Am I talking to Josie McIntyre?" he demanded.

"No, you're talking to Josie Moore. Since I got married, I've learned discretion."

"Yeah, right," Matt said with a chuckle. He loved his sister, but he knew better than to believe that claim. But he had something else on his mind.

"Listen, you and Justin are coming for Thanksgiving dinner, aren't you?"

"Of course we are."

"I talked to Jeff while I was in town today. He and Bailey are coming. I want you to ask Annie, too. You and Justin could pick her up."

"Good idea, Matt. I don't want her to be alone."

No, he didn't, either. Especially when he felt Alex's departure was partly his fault. "Yeah. And why not ask Dr. Lee to join us? There's always room for one more at the table."

"That's a great idea. I'll talk to both of them tomorrow."

"Good. Don't let her drive by herself. Pick her up, too."

"Yes, master."

"Watch it, short stuff, or you'll have to do all the dishes by yourself."

"I don't think I can stand on my feet that long, Matt, since I'm pregnant," she said calmly.

"I was kidding, Josie. You know I didn't mean it."

"I was kidding, too, Matt. Being pregnant doesn't make me a wimp."

His sister could drive him crazy. "Go do some work before Justin fires you." She helped her husband with the local newspaper.

"Right. I'll talk to you soon."

He hung up the phone and turned to go back outside. He had more work to do.

"You invitin' Annie for Thanksgiving?" Willie asked as she scrubbed the kitchen counter.

Matt suddenly realized he should let his cook know how many to prepare for. "Yeah, Annie and the doctor."

"Dr. Dave?"

"No, Dr. Lee, the OB-GYN. Is that okay?"

"'Course it is. She's a nice lady. And pregnant."

"Yeah."

As he crossed the yard to the barns, he told himself that was the best reason for him to avoid the woman. She was pregnant. But she was also alone.

That bothered him. Justin was taking care of Josie, and Jeff would hardly let Bailey out of his sight, Alex had left, but the family kept an eye on Annie. But who was going to care for Elizabeth? Dr. Lee, he amended, though it seemed silly to be so formal when he'd already held her in his arms.

Not as a lover, of course. But she was little, a lot smaller than Julie who—

He came to an abrupt halt. He hadn't thought about Julie in a while. She'd been the perfect wife for a rancher, a homebody who loved to cook and clean, knit and sew. She'd even helped around the ranch, so eager was she to be at his side.

She'd been perfect.

He shook his head and strode on toward the barns. He didn't have time to stand around.

EVEN WILLIE WENT to the Thanksgiving Fair.

Sunday was the day when work was lightest on the ranch. Only the absolute necessities were done, feeding the animals in the barn, making sure the cows on the range had hay and holes were chopped in the ice for water.

Matt had seen that all of that had been done before breakfast. He'd attended church, as usual, and Willie had left lunch in the refrigerator for him. Matt didn't want to sit down and eat alone. He felt restless today.

Suddenly he knew what he intended to do. Changing into jeans, he grabbed a snow shovel and tossed it into the back of his truck. Then he drove into Bison City.

First he stopped at Annie's house. She lived alone next to her office. As the local veterinarian, she did a booming business, though her uncle, who'd retired earlier, had taken over again until her baby was born.

Like Elizabeth's, Annie's sidewalk was covered with snow. Matt shrugged off his coat and set to work. An hour later he surveyed the results of his efforts. Annie's sidewalk was cleared of snow and was now drying in the sunshine.

Next he drove to Dr. Lee's house. He knew that the doctor, along with Annie, Josie and all the pregnant ladies in town, would be at the Thanksgiving Fair. No one would know who shoveled the snow.

He repeated his actions until Elizabeth's sidewalk, too, was drying in the sun. No slippery snow for a pregnant lady to fall on.

As he was standing there, he noticed several shingles missing on the roof. Though any precipitation would be in the form of snow for the next four months, the sun would melt the snow after each storm and the melted snow could do damage to her house.

He'd have to do something about the leaks...at least on the outside. She'd be at the office during the week. He could take care of it without her knowing.

Yeah, that's what he'd do. He could help take care of her without her knowing. He wouldn't have to be around her, talk to her, touch her. Whoa! Where had that come from? Of course he wouldn't touch her.

He was just going to fix her roof.

ELIZABETH WAS EXHAUSTED. The Thanksgiving Fair was a complete success, earning much more money for the hospital than even optimistic Josie had hoped for. It seemed the happiness of the expectant mothers was spreading to all of Bison City and beyond.

She rubbed her tummy as her baby kicked. "Easy there, Sarah. Mommy's tired. Let's take it easy."

As if that plea would be met. Her baby sometimes seemed to be a gymnastics star.

She turned into her driveway, glad to be home. It wasn't until she'd gotten out of the car and started up her sidewalk that she noticed the lack of snow.

Coming to an abrupt halt, she stared at the dry cement. Then she looked at her neighbors' sidewalks. Maybe a good neighbor had cleared her sidewalk when they'd done theirs. But no, their sidewalks were still buried in five inches of snow.

Matt McIntyre.

It had to be him. With a sigh she continued into the house. He must've been a wonderful husband, assuming his wife wanted to be smothered with care.

She put on the teakettle, sat down by the phone and, after looking up the number for the McIntyre ranch, dialed it.

"McIntyre," a gruff voice answered.

She recognized his voice. "Thank you for clearing my sidewalk."

He said nothing.

"Matt? I said—"

"I heard you. How'd you know it was me?"

"I don't know anyone else who wasn't at the Thanksgiving Fair. It was thoughtful of you."

"I don't want you to fall."

"I know. You must've done a good job of taking care of Julie." She'd deliberately used his wife's name, knowing it would shock him.

"How do you know her name?" he barked.

"Josie mentioned it. I'm sorry about her death. My husband died recently, too."

She thought he wasn't going to respond. Finally he said, "Did he know you were pregnant?"

"No," she admitted with a sigh.

"What happened?" His abrupt questions were an attempt to hide his emotions, but Elizabeth could hear them in the sexy burr.

"He got a rare disease, one you wouldn't know about, and died a week later."

"But you're a doctor!" Matt protested.

Elizabeth had spent a lot of time dealing with that very thing. She was a good doctor, but she wasn't a miracle worker.

"I'm sorry, I didn't mean…" Matt began, filling the silence.

"No, it's all right. I couldn't save him."

"I'm sorry."

"Me, too. He was a good man. Just as I'm sure Julie was a good woman."

"I should've protected her," Matt muttered.

"And I should've cured Dale. But I couldn't, and you couldn't save Julie."

"It's different with me. If I'd been driving, I might've avoided—"

"Matt, it was an accident. Would it help if you'd died, too? You know you're important to your family." Josie and her brothers spoke of Matt with affection and respect. He'd been running the family ranch for eight years.

"I don't know why we're talking about this," he said with a growl, showing his displeasure.

"Because keeping your sorrow penned up isn't healthy. You can't get on with your life if you don't let go."

"Mind your own business, Doc. I'm not a patient!"

"Sorry, I'm afraid it's hard to stop being a doctor after hours. Kind of like being a rancher. If your cows need you at midnight, I bet you don't tell them to wait until morning."

"That's different."

"I'm not sure it is. But I won't keep you any longer. I just wanted to say thank-you."

She expected him to hang up at once. Instead, he had another question.

"Did Josie talk to you about Thursday?"

"She invited me to Thanksgiving dinner. Is it still okay if I come?"

"Why wouldn't it be? Josie can ask whomever she wants. This is her home, too."

Elizabeth knew the invitation had come from Matt. But it was all right if he didn't want to admit that.

"Then, thank you. I'd love to come. What shall I bring?"

"There's no need to bring anything."

"I'd really like to contribute to the dinner," she insisted.

"Okay," he agreed with an exasperated sigh, "you can bake something for dessert. Willie doesn't much like to bake."

"Oh. Okay, of course." She hoped Matt couldn't hear the panic in her voice. She seldom cooked, and the last time she'd tried to bake a cake, for Dale's last birthday, it had been a disaster.

"I like cherry pie."

A pie? Pie crust? "I'll see what I can do," she said with more confidence than she had any hope of having.

"Annie's coming, too. Justin will drive all of you."

"I can drive myself. If I got a call, I'd have to

leave, and I wouldn't want to cut short anyone else's pleasure.''

"They'd call you on Thanksgiving?"

"Remember your cows? Won't you take care of them on Thanksgiving?"

"Yeah, but on my own schedule."

"Well, babies don't like schedules."

"Okay, I'll come pick you up."

"Don't be silly. I'll drive myself—"

"No! The road might be slick. I'll pick you up at eleven. Be ready." And he hung up the phone.

"Well, really!" Elizabeth exclaimed as she replaced the receiver. The man was impossible.

But her biggest problem was the cherry pie. She'd never made a pie in her entire life.

What was she going to do now?

Chapter Three

Now that she was six to eight weeks away from delivery, Elizabeth was trying to shorten her office hours. She only saw her pregnancy patients, leaving any other problems to Dave Gardner, the general practitioner with whom she shared an office.

Thanksgiving week she'd taken even fewer appointments than usual. Only four women had appointments on Monday, so Elizabeth planned a relaxing afternoon, studying cookbooks. After all, she was a doctor. She could follow directions for a recipe.

So why hadn't she been able to follow the directions on the back of a cake mix box? Because she kept getting distracted, she finally admitted. Somehow it was difficult to concentrate on a mix when she had a patient in trouble.

Like Barbie Ward. Barbie was due December ninth. But after her examination today, Elizabeth was worried. She should've insisted that Barbie go to bed and stay there, but the woman had a large family coming for Thanksgiving. She'd pleaded to be allowed to prepare for her guests.

Elizabeth hadn't had a good reason to put her patient to bed. Only a feeling. Barbie had promised to rest frequently. With Barbie on her mind, Elizabeth pulled into her driveway without seeing her house.

Until she heard a noise from above her as she got out.

A man was on her roof, hammering.

She recognized him immediately. No one else had those broad shoulders and narrow hips. Or maybe it was the square jaw that told her who was on her roof. "Matt McIntyre, what are you doing up there?"

He looked over his shoulder, frowning. "What are you doing home now?"

As if it was her fault he was up there. "I've shortened my hours. Why are you up there?"

"You had some shingles off. If they're not fixed, you'll have a leak soon." Then he turned back around and began hammering again.

"I'll hire someone. Come down before you fall." He ignored her.

"Matt McIntyre, come down right now. I insist."

"Go on in and make yourself some tea. I'll be finished in just a minute."

Elizabeth clenched her hands into fists. The man was so stubborn. She marched into the house, determined not to try to save him from himself ever again.

She fixed her tea and sat down on the sofa, putting her feet up on the coffee table. If she stood on her feet too long, her ankles would swell.

And she listened to Matt moving around on her roof.

She didn't realize how tense she was, as if waiting for him to fall, until he knocked on the front door. With a deep sigh, she called, "Come in."

The big man came into her house, filling the room with his energy. "The roof's all fixed."

"Thank you. But if you'd told me my roof needed fixing, I would've hired someone. There was no need to interrupt your work schedule."

"I needed to come to town, anyway," he said with a shrug. "How are you feeling?"

"A little tired. Sarah's getting heavy."

"Have you had lunch?"

"No, not yet. I'll make something after I've rested a little," she assured him.

Without answering, he walked past her into the kitchen.

"What are you doing?" she called, unwilling to go through the struggle of rising.

He came back into the living room. "You don't have anything worth having in your refrigerator."

"There's a frozen dinner in the top."

"That's not healthy for the baby. I'll be back in a minute." And he walked out the front door.

Now what was he up to? The man never took no for an answer. But she was too tired to worry about Matt McIntyre right now. Sarah had been particularly active last night, and Elizabeth hadn't had much sleep. She lay her head on the back of the sofa and closed her eyes.

She'd rest just a couple of minutes. Then she'd get up and fix some lunch.

MATT RAPPED ON THE front door when he returned, but he didn't wait for Elizabeth to open the door. He remembered how hard it had been for Julie to get up.

Good thing he hadn't waited, he decided, since he found Elizabeth curled up on the sofa, sound asleep. He continued through to the kitchen and began setting out the food he'd bought from the Chuck Wagon Café. Nell's food was basic, nothing fancy, but it was good for you.

He found silverware in a drawer, then filled glasses with milk. Pregnant ladies were supposed to drink a lot of milk. He'd bought some at the drive-in grocery. He even set out the napkins Nell had stuffed into the sack.

Then he went back to the living room.

"Elizabeth, lunch is ready," he called, keeping his distance.

She stirred but didn't come awake.

"Elizabeth?" he called, moving a step closer.

Finally he did what he'd hoped to avoid. He touched her, gently shaking her shoulder. "Elizabeth, come eat."

"What?" she muttered, her eyelids fluttering.

"Lunch is ready."

She struggled to a sitting position and blinked several times. "You cooked?"

"No, there wasn't anything here to cook. I went to the Chuck Wagon. The special today is meat loaf."

Her eyes lit up with enthusiasm, which amused him. Her cupboard wasn't bare because of a lack of interest in eating, at least. "Come on."

She held out a hand. "Could you help me?"

Which meant he had to touch her again. But how could he refuse? He grasped her hand and reached for the other one. Then he hauled her up from the couch...right into his arms.

"Oh, sorry," she murmured, her hands coming to rest on his chest as his arms went around her. "I'm a little unsteady on my feet."

He stepped back. "Understandable," he assured her. And reminded himself to keep his distance. Gesturing with his hand, he pointed her in the direction of the kitchen. "I set the table in there."

"Are you going to join me?" she asked, before she moved.

"Yeah, if you don't mind. I haven't had lunch yet, either."

Her smile radiated warmth, as if the sun had come from behind a cloud. He took another step back. Maybe he was making a mistake here.

He had no choice, now that he'd told her he was going to eat with her. To leave would be the height of rudeness. So he followed her to the kitchen, holding her chair for her as she sat down, then taking his place opposite her.

"Ooh, I love Nell's meat loaf," she enthused

after they'd asked a brief blessing. "Thank you, Matt."

"So you've eaten at the Chuck Wagon before?"

She laughed. "I guess. I'm a regular customer. A lot of times I stop off there before I come home."

"Well, I'm glad you're getting some decent food somewhere. Don't you ever grocery shop?"

She shrugged her shoulders as if it didn't matter. "Yes, of course, but…but lately, I've been kind of tired, so I keep putting it off."

"You need someone to help. Why haven't you hired a housekeeper? You can afford one, with all the pregnant ladies around here."

"I'm trying to find someone who can help with Sarah after she's born and maybe do a little house-keeping. But it's not easy."

"So you're not going to stay home and take care of your baby?" He tried to keep the censure out of his voice, but he couldn't. Julie had looked forward to devoting herself to their son.

"I'm a doctor, Matt. Would you give up your cows, if your child had lived?"

"Of course not, but that's my job," he protested, frowning.

"Being a doctor is my job."

"But if your husband had lived, to support you, you would've stayed home?"

"No." She didn't soften her response or try to justify it, which irritated Matt.

"So you don't care about your baby!" he returned, angry.

Elizabeth shoved her chair back from the table and started the time-consuming process of rising.

Matt leaped from his seat and rounded the table to put a hand on her shoulder, forcing her to stay seated.

She glared up at him. "Don't you ever say such a thing again. I love my baby!"

"Then why would you not take care of her?"

She closed her eyes and turned her face away. "Being a doctor is who I am. It's a gift I have. Sarah wouldn't want me to be less than I can be."

"Sarah won't understand that until she's at least in her twenties. How do you explain that to a child?"

"I won't have to explain it. All Sarah will care about is that she's loved and cared for. It may not always be me feeding her and changing her every time, but it will be someone who cares about her."

"How do you know? I've seen those shows on television where parents think their child is well cared for. Then they put in a hidden camera and they discover the baby is being mistreated."

ELIZABETH GROANED. She'd seen those shows, too. "That's one of the reasons I moved to Bison City. It's less likely to happen in a small town because everyone knows his neighbor. I'm only going to hire someone who has recommendations."

"Are you going to eat?" he asked, still standing beside her chair.

She nodded and watched as he returned to his seat. When he sat down, he continued their conversation as if he hadn't interrupted it. "I suppose that's good, but you have to be careful."

"I know that."

She took a bite of the heavenly meat loaf and chewed it slowly. She didn't want to think about her problems right now. She was too tired.

"Julie wanted to take care of our baby herself."

There were a lot of things Elizabeth could've said. That Julie may have burned out if she didn't have help. That their marriage may have suffered if she dedicated herself completely to their baby. That she might have had difficulty taking care of herself. But Elizabeth couldn't criticize Matt's wife when the woman never had a chance to care for her child. "Good for her."

She kept her head down, concentrating on her meal.

"Of course, Willie was there to help."

"Who's Willie?"

"Her name is actually Wilhemena Brown. She came to work for me when Mom and Dad moved to Florida. She's the housekeeper."

"A housekeeper is a luxury a lot of mothers don't have." But one she was considering. "I don't suppose Willie would want to come to work for me?" She shot Matt a teasing smile.

"Don't even think about it. My refrigerator would look like yours without Willie around."

"Ah. So you're no better at taking care of yourself than I am?"

"Probably not, but I'm busy. A ranch takes a lot of work."

Somebody needed to educate the man about a woman's life. "So do pregnant doctors."

He grimaced and said, "I guess you're right. Is that why you're so tired today?"

With a sigh she admitted, "Sarah wasn't sleepy last night, unlike her mother. She played soccer or something most of the night, so I didn't get much sleep."

"Soccer? Your little girl is going to play soccer?"

"Don't they play it here? It's very popular in Dallas."

"There's not much soccer played around here. The snow kind of keeps the fields useless until late May, early June."

"It lasts that long? But it's only November. You mean we'll have snow continuously until May?" She couldn't imagine that much winter.

"Didn't you check things out before you moved?" he asked, an eyebrow sliding up.

He had the sexiest face, she thought dreamily, before snapping herself back from that thought. "Um, sort of. Dave said—"

"Dr. Gardner?"

"Yes. He moved here from Cheyenne a couple of years ago, but we'd worked together in Dallas a while back. He said the winters weren't too bad."

Matt nodded in agreement. "They aren't. But we have a lot of snow. And we need it. It keeps things from getting too dry." His gaze fell to her plate. "You need to eat a little more."

Elizabeth had managed about half her meal. Considering the portions Nell served, she thought that was pretty good. "I'm full. I'll put it in the refrigerator and reheat it for dinner."

He grunted, but she wasn't sure if that was agreement or disgust. "Okay. Go lie down. I'll clean up and let myself out."

"No, that's not necessary. You brought lunch. I can clean up the kitchen. And I need to pay you for—"

"Don't even think about it."

His hardened tones stopped her as much as his words. "Don't think about what?"

"Paying for lunch."

"But why shouldn't I? You—"

"It was my decision, and I pay." He rose from his chair and began opening drawers, distracting her.

"What are you doing now?"

"Looking for foil to cover your leftovers."

"Second drawer to the left," she directed, before he'd searched her entire kitchen.

With admirable efficiency, he covered her plate with foil, placed it in the refrigerator and put his empty plate in the sink. "You need to drink all your milk."

She rolled her eyes. "I know that, Matt. I'm the one who directs the other pregnant women, remember?"

"I remember. But I think you don't follow all the rules with yourself."

She upended her glass to prove him wrong. "There. Satisfied?"

"Yup," he agreed, and took her glass to the sink to rinse it as well as his own. Then he faced her again.

"Now, come on. Let's get you to bed."

Her eyes widened as his words called up improbable images. Shaking off thoughts of the two of them in bed, she raised her chin and said, "What do you mean, 'let's'?"

"Don't worry. I'm not going to undress you. I figure for a nap you can sleep in what you've got on, but you may need help getting into bed."

Matt and a bed were a lethal combination. She looked away. Where were these thoughts coming from? She wasn't interested in Matt as a man. She was only interested in him as a patient. A patient who seemed determined to treat *her* as one.

"I can manage just fine," she assured him.

Of course she hadn't included standing. Before she could get to her feet, two strong hands lifted her. "Matt! I can do it."

"I see no point in you straining when I'm around to help. Where's the bedroom?"

"I need to lock the door after you leave. Then I'll go to bed." She needed to lock the door to her heart, too. This man, with his caring and his sexiness, could undermine a woman's resistance in no time.

"Nope. I'll lock it behind me. If you don't lie down now, you'll find a reason not to. Come on. I'm not leaving you until I know you're going to get some rest."

"Do you realize how ridiculous this is?" she

protested. "You just met me Saturday, and you think you have the right to boss me around?"

"Look, Elizabeth, it's for your own good. You don't have anyone to take care of you. Josie doesn't need me, or Bailey. We're all helping Annie. But you're alone. I'm just being neighborly."

"I think you're taking *neighborly* a little too far."

"Do you want me to carry you to bed?"

They were standing practically nose to nose, except that hers was almost a foot below his. She had no doubt that he would scoop her up in his strong arms and do exactly as he said. She didn't want that. Of course she didn't.

A tremor ran through her and she turned her back, walking away from him with as much grace as she could muster. "I'm going to bed. Goodbye."

He followed her.

"Matt! You can't come into my bedroom."

He said nothing, but he didn't stop.

She whirled around, almost toppling over. He reached out to steady her. "Look, my bedroom is a mess. I was too tired to make my bed."

With a grin, his hands stroking her arms, he returned, "I didn't make mine this morning, either."

"Right. But I bet Willie did." She was trying to keep her thoughts on the mundane, but his touch was distracting.

"Yep. So you need to get a housekeeper. I'll ask Willie if she knows of anyone."

"That kind of help I'll gladly take. Thank you. Now, go away."

"As soon as you're in bed."

She gave up. Okay, so he saw she was a slob. Maybe that would send him on his way. She entered her bedroom, almost groaning aloud at the discarded clothing on the floor, the unmade bed, the dust on her dresser.

Lately it had all become just a little too much for her.

"I told you it was a mess," she muttered, embarrassed.

"I've seen worse," he assured her, his smile gentle and encouraging. "Sit down and I'll slip your shoes off," he offered.

She was wearing slip-ons because untying sneakers caused too much work. Before she could assure him she could manage, he was on one knee, reaching for her feet.

"You've got a little swelling. Is that normal?"

He was still trying to play doctor. She tried to resent it, but the warmth of his big hands on her feet felt heavenly. "Yes, considering the lack of sleep and the fact that I'm six to eight weeks before delivery."

"Want a foot massage?"

"No!" she replied, jerking her feet from his gentle touch. That was the last thing she needed. But a heavenly thought.

"How about a back rub? Julie—some pregnant women have backaches."

"Thanks for offering, but I'm fine." God was making it tough on her, having to turn down both a foot massage and a back rub. But she had to. She didn't need the complication of Matt touching her. She drew her feet to the bed and reclined against the pillow.

Matt lifted the cover, pulling it over her. "Do you need to loosen your clothing?"

"Are you going to offer to help?" she demanded belligerently. Really, the man was going too far. Or not far enough. That thought shot panic through her veins. She was pregnant! What was wrong with her?

"Nope. I'm on my way out of here," he assured her, but there was a twinkle in his blue gaze that tempted her to smile back. "Sleep tight," he added as he approached the door.

"Thank you," she muttered, still irritated with him. Yet the care he gave her soothed a feeling of neglect, of loneliness, that none of her lady friends' help had been able to do for her.

She was *not* one of those women who needed a man to feel complete. She wasn't.

But Matt McIntyre would satisfy any woman's wish list for a good man.

MATT WAS BACK half an hour later. He let himself in the unlocked door without knocking. He didn't want to disrupt Elizabeth's nap.

In his arms he carried several sacks from the local grocery store. He put away the gallon of milk, the fresh bread, fruit, instant oatmeal. He'd heard oatmeal was good for everyone, and instant should be easy even for the doctor.

He'd bought a few other basics and a couple of

treats, some chocolate. He knew Annie swore by chocolate.

After everything had been put away, he couldn't resist tiptoeing back to Elizabeth's bed. He stood beside it, watching her breathe deeply, her cheeks flushed with sleep.

She was a hardheaded little thing, not at all like Julie. In fact, they couldn't be more opposite. So she wasn't a woman he'd ever be interested in. The need to protect her, provide for her, could be explained by her need, not his. He could offer her that protection.

Just until the baby was born.

Before he left, he bent down and barely brushed her cheek with his lips. As a friend.

'Cause she wasn't the lady for him. There would never be anyone for him but Julie. But Elizabeth needed him. And being needed again felt good.

Chapter Four

By Thanksgiving morning the snow had melted, the sun was shining, and Matt was in a good mood. He loved family get-togethers.

A momentary frown filled his face. Alex wouldn't be there. Which really wasn't unusual. The boy had a wanderlust that frequently took him away from home. But Matt still felt guilty for Alex's absence this year.

He should be here...for Annie.

A man should always be there to protect his lady when she was pregnant. His frown deepened as he immediately pictured Elizabeth Lee. Sometimes a man couldn't be, like Elizabeth's husband. But Alex was alive.

His happy mood now thoroughly chased away, Matt hurried through the essential chores, his coat collar turned up against the cold wind.

When he came back into the kitchen, he grabbed a mug and filled it from the coffeepot Willie always had ready.

"Cold enough for you?" Willie asked while she basted the big turkey.

"Yeah." They had the same conversation most mornings. Matt found it comforting that some things never changed. He leaned against the kitchen counter, sipping the hot liquid.

"Annie called. Asked if Dex could come to dinner, too. Said she hated to ask, but she couldn't leave him alone on Thanksgiving." Though Dex was known for his crusty attitude, he'd raised his niece and had been the local vet until Annie took over.

Matt looked at Willie. "I assume you said yes."

"A'course. He's almost family."

Matt hid his smile behind his coffee cup. Family was everything to Willie. And the McIntyres were her family. "Good."

"She said Dex would drive her, so I guess Josie and Justin can pick up Dr. Lee, and you won't have to drive into town," Willie continued, her gaze fastened on the big bird.

Matt was grateful for Willie's attention to her cooking. That way she wouldn't see how her words upset him. Which was ridiculous. He should be glad he didn't have to make a trip into town.

"Uh, I was going to pick her up in case she got a call. She shouldn't be driving on an emergency call while she's pregnant," he pointed out, avoiding Willie's look as she turned to stare at him.

"If she gets a call while she's here, I reckon you could drive her. That'd be neighborly," Willie said with a nod, as if that decided the matter.

He guessed it did. "Did you call Josie and tell her?"

"I did. She's bringing your mother's famous stuffing. I think she made four pans of it."

"Good."

"Bailey called and said she's bringing a cake. That girl can surely bake."

It had taken Willie a while to accept Bailey, since Jeff's lady hadn't been sure she could settle in Wyoming when she'd dreamed of being in New York. But Bailey's cooking skills, as well as her love for Jeff, had won Willie over.

"You've had a busy morning on the phone," Matt commented, continuing to drink his coffee and thaw out.

"Yep. Annie's bringing potato salad."

"Uh, the doctor wanted to know what to bring. I suggested a cherry pie."

Willie stared at him before turning back to the turkey. "Yep. Always was your favorite."

Matt decided it was time to escape the kitchen. Willie's stare made him nervous. Always had. "I'm going to catch up on some paperwork."

"Ah-huh," Willie agreed.

He could feel her gaze on his back as he hurried out the door.

ELIZABETH STARED at the perfect cherry pie sitting on her kitchen table. And felt guilty.

She hadn't baked it.

Oh, she'd tried. The results had been thrown out, since no one, not even a dog, would've wanted a piece of the hard, lumpy crust or the watery pie filling. She'd called Josie in a panic yesterday, determined not to go to the family dinner.

Josie had firmly refused to let her out of her commitment. "We're not asking you to come because we love cherry pie," she'd said.

"Matt is."

"Maybe. But that's his problem."

"Josie, you're making something, aren't you? And I know Annie is. Bailey is a good cook so she'll make something spectacular. I simply can't be the only woman to turn up empty-handed. It would be so humiliating." Dale had gently teased her about her lack of culinary skills, but he'd also appreciated her other talents.

The McIntyres, or rather Matt McIntyre, wouldn't have that balanced a view.

"Look, Elizabeth, if you're worried about it, call Nell."

"Nell? At the Chuck Wagon Café?"

"Yeah. She makes the best pies in the world. Especially cherry ones. I won't tell where you got it from."

So Elizabeth had called Nell, and now she had a perfect cherry pie. But she wasn't going to pretend she'd made it. That would be dishonest.

When the rap on her front door alerted her that her ride had come, she hurried to the front of the house, a surprising eagerness filling her. It was because she was going to a family gathering, she assured herself.

She didn't often have that opportunity. What remained of her family lived in a small town in south Texas. Some aunts, a cousin or two.

So what explained the disappointment that filled her when she discovered Justin on the doorstep? "Hi. Is everything all right?" She looked over his shoulder to see Josie sitting in the SUV he drove.

"Everything's fine. We're saving Matt a drive into town." Justin, as handsome as the McIntyre men, only not quite as dark and intense, smiled.

"Maybe I should follow you with my car. I might have to leave on a call," she offered, trying to maintain her smile.

"Nope. If you need to leave, one of us will drive you. Matt was adamant about that." He held the door open for her.

"Do all of you do exactly what Matt says to do?" She didn't really wait for an answer. She thought she already knew it.

"Most of us. Alex rebels sometimes. But in the end Matt's usually right."

"How irritating," she said with a smile, sailing past him with her perfect cherry pie in her arms.

"Yeah," Justin agreed with a chuckle. "Josie particularly finds it bothersome."

Once they were in the vehicle, Josie looked at her and said, "So, you made a pie? What kind is it?"

Elizabeth shook her head. "I'm not going to pretend, Josie. You know I bought it from Nell."

"Hey, Nell's pies are my favorites," Justin proclaimed. "Is it a blueberry?"

"No, cherry."

Justin slanted her a quick look over his shoulder. "Oh. Matt's favorite."

Her cheeks burned. "He suggested cherry. Doesn't anyone else like it?"

"We all love it," Josie assured her. "But Matt is crazy about cherry pie. Julie always made it for him."

Elizabeth's heart sank. She should've known. Well, she wasn't competing with the dead Julie. She wasn't interested in Matt McIntyre other than as a patient, so it didn't matter if he thought she was a total klutz in the kitchen.

It didn't matter at all.

ANNIE AND HER UNCLE DEX arrived at the same time as Justin, Josie and Elizabeth. In the rush of greetings, Elizabeth slipped the pie plate holding the much-discussed cherry pie unobtrusively onto the kitchen counter.

Willie, however, saw her.

"You bake that?"

Good thing Elizabeth had already decided what her answer would be. "No. I bought it from Nell. I'm not good in the kitchen, but I didn't want to come empty-handed."

Willie gave her a sharp look, but only nodded her head.

When they were all seated around the big table, the magnificent turkey sitting in front of Matt, and the table crowded with fragrant dishes, the conversation turned to the baby contest, the Millennium Baby.

"You wouldn't believe the number of requests we've gotten in the mail this week," Bailey said. "We're going to make a lot of money for the hospital, Elizabeth."

"That's wonderful. You've all done an incredible job." Elizabeth had thought they would make a couple of hundred dollars, at best. Which wouldn't add much to the bare-bones hospital. But a news crew had interviewed the pregnant ladies of Bison City at the Thanksgiving Fair and suddenly they were getting interest from all over Wyoming.

She would've given her support to their efforts in any case, but she was growing excited about the possibility of upgrading the hospital to a fully staffed, well-prepared medical facility.

"It's certainly keeping us busy," Josie complained, but her smile belied her words.

"As long as you get plenty of rest, that's good. It keeps you from counting the days," Elizabeth assured her, smiling. "Makes time pass faster."

"Any word from Alex?" Matt asked abruptly, drawing everyone's attention as he stared at Annie.

Annie smiled serenely. "No, not yet. But he'll be back. He and Koby have some work to do," she said, naming the cutting horse Alex was training somewhere down in Texas. She took a bite of turkey, ignoring everyone's stare.

Josie voiced her irritation. "I can't believe he just up and left. That was a rotten thing to do."

Several people started to speak, but Annie stopped them before they could second Josie's words.

"Alex has some things to work out, but I believe in him. And in Koby." She turned to look at Matt, as if speaking expressly to him.

Elizabeth watched as Matt inhaled deeply. But he didn't blast Annie. In fact, he offered an apology. "You're right. I'm probably the reason he left. I didn't have a lot of faith in the horse...or in Alex's decisions. I'm sorry, Annie."

"I didn't, either," Annie said softly, "but I have to believe he'll be back."

Willie tried to dispel the awkward moment. "Eat up, folks. We've still got Bailey's scrumptious chocolate cake and a cherry pie to do away with."

MATT'S GAZE immediately went to Elizabeth. She'd made a cherry pie. Just like Julie. It probably wouldn't be as good, of course, because Julie had been an incredible cook, but he appreciated the effort.

It was almost like a sign. If he could help Elizabeth deliver her baby safely, maybe he wouldn't continue to bear the heavy burden of guilt for failing to protect his wife and child.

He knew he was being ridiculous. It was far too much weight to put on a cherry pie, but it seemed symbolic.

When dessert was served, he voiced his preference for the cherry pie. The first bite almost melted in his mouth. The doctor did have some skills in the kitchen.

"Incredible pie, Elizabeth," he praised, smiling at her.

''Thank you. I'll tell Nell,'' she said, smiling in return.

The remains of the pie in his mouth turned to tasteless dust. ''What? Why would you—''

''I bought the pie from Nell. I told you I don't cook well.''

Everyone at the table seemed to be staring at him, but Matt ignored them. He deliberately put down his fork and shoved his slice of pie away. ''That wasn't necessary.''

He hadn't meant to be rude. And Elizabeth didn't act as if his words had upset her. She stared at him, her hazel eyes calm.

But the rest of those gathered around the table must've thought he was rude, because there was a flurry of compliments and jokes to cover the awkward silence.

Matt picked up his coffee cup for something to do. At least the moment had passed. He would just pretend the cherry pie in front of him didn't exist.

''I understand Julie was an incredible cook. Were her pies better than Nell's?'' Elizabeth asked.

Matt froze. His family didn't discuss Julie. He'd made it clear to them that Julie was not to be talked about. What was wrong with the woman? Was she incredibly insensitive?

To his surprise Josie answered. ''Yeah, Julie could cook circles around anyone in the county. She always won a blue ribbon at the local fair, right, Matt?'' She looked at him, appearing nervous but determined.

He nodded. It was all he could do. Speaking wasn't an option.

"Do you remember that quilt she made for the baby?" Annie asked, not looking in Matt's direction. "It won a blue ribbon, too. Mrs. Appleton offered her two hundred dollars for it. She wanted it for her grandbaby."

He remembered the quilt. It was packed away, along with the blue ribbons and all the mementos of his happy life. Packed away with his happiness.

"She sounds like a very talented lady," Elizabeth said softly.

Matt couldn't take it any longer. He stood up so quickly his chair tipped over. "I'm going to the barn." And he stomped out of the room.

Silence prevailed until the back door slammed shut, announcing Matt's exit.

"What's wrong with all of you?" Jeff asked, staring around the table. "You know Matt doesn't like to talk about Julie."

"But he has to," Josie said, leaning forward. "He's getting more and more remote. All the baby stuff is hurting him."

"So what does talking about Julie do? Make it only hurt more?" Jeff demanded, angry with his baby sister. "That was cruel, Josie."

Her eyes filled with tears, and Justin wrapped his arm around her shoulders. "Back off, Jeff," Justin ordered as he comforted his wife.

"I don't—" Jeff began, his voice raised.

"It's my fault," Elizabeth said, interrupting him. When she had everyone's attention, including a distraught Willie, she said, "Matt has buried his anger and remorse about Julie and the baby for too long. If he doesn't talk about them, he's going to grow more and more remote until the pain is too much to bear. I encouraged Josie to talk about Julie in front of him. I'm sorry."

Annie concurred. "You're right, Elizabeth. Josie and I discussed what you said. Matt is such a good man. He deserves to be happy."

Jeff wasn't convinced. "Amateurs trying to play doctor! Leave Matt alone."

"I don't think we can all be called amateurs," Bailey replied calmly, "since Elizabeth is a doctor."

Jeff whirled around to stare at his beloved. "You're siding with them?"

"It's not a question of—" Bailey began.

Dex, having remained silent, lumbered to his feet, interrupting her. "I'm going to the barn. Matt might have an animal or two that needs looking at. Might as well have a look-see while I'm here."

Jeff stood. "Sounds good to me. Matt might like some company." Then he turned to his brother-in-law. "You coming, Justin?"

Justin leaned over and kissed his wife's forehead. Then said, "I guess I'd better join the guys, sweetheart, before I'm labeled a turncoat."

"Fine," Josie returned, though her voice told him it wasn't fine at all. "We'll leave the dishes for you men. After all, it's too much for Willie by herself, and we're all pregnant."

"Uh, okay," Justin said, shooting an alarmed

look at Jeff as he joined him near the door. "That'll be fine."

Then the two men ran for their lives.

After several moments of silence, Elizabeth said, "I'm sorry. I didn't intend to ruin a lovely Thanksgiving dinner."

Willie, who was fiercely loyal to the McIntyres, turned to her, and Elizabeth held her breath. Probably the woman would lambaste her for what had happened.

"Is it true? Is Matt gonna explode?"

Elizabeth reached out to cover the work-worn hand of the older lady. "I can't say for sure. But he can't get on with his life until he deals with the past. At least not successfully. Josie said she'd been teasing him about marrying again. But I don't believe that will happen unless he accepts Julie's and the baby's deaths."

Willie sighed. "Lord have mercy, he's going to be angry."

"But, Willie," Josie pleaded, "I want Matt to marry, to have his own children. What happened was an accident, but he blames himself."

Willie stood up and began clearing the table. "You're right," she agreed, carrying several platters to the counter.

"I am?" Josie replied, a comical expression of surprise on her face.

Willie turned and stared at all the ladies at the table. "Yep. I've been waiting, hoping—but he's a stubborn man. A good man, but a stubborn one."

Annie picked up several bowls and joined Willie. "We were just trying to help."

"Yep. And Dr. Lee, I thank you. That boy needs a good woman. Someone to help him out around here. I won't live forever." Willie lifted a corner of the apron she wore and wiped the corner of one eye.

Immediately all four pregnant ladies formed a circle around Willie for a group hug. It wasn't easy since their stomachs didn't allow for close quarters, but it was definitely a hug.

MATT WAS ANGRY. So angry he kicked the barn door after he closed it. "Ow!" he complained and hobbled over to a nearby bench. The horses stirred at the noise, several of them sticking their heads out of their stalls.

He should've been more careful. Those mares were being kept in the barn because they were due to give birth soon. Expectant mothers needed peace and quiet.

Expectant mothers.

A picture of Julie formed in his mind. She'd been so proud of her protruding stomach, so thrilled to be carrying their baby.

It wasn't fair! That childish protest sprang into his mind, and he cursed under his breath. No, it wasn't fair. But then, who'd promised fairness?

He knew he was sinking into self-pity. He hated self-pity. That was why he'd put his anger, his sadness behind him, hidden it away. He was the oldest of his siblings. He was the boss on the large ranch. He was a man.

He didn't like feeling weak, helpless...alone.

The barn door opened.

His head snapped up. If Elizabeth had— It wasn't Elizabeth, but it was disturbing that she'd been his first thought.

"Dex! Need something?" He had to clear his throat, as if he hadn't spoken in a while.

"Nah. Just wanted to move around after a big meal. The ladies doing okay?"

Matt thought he was asking about the human ladies in the house who'd just stirred up a lot of trouble. Then he realized Dex was referring to the mares. He should've known. Dex didn't talk about much except animals.

"They're fine. I don't think it'll be long before Missy foals."

"I'll look at her," Dex said, heading for the second stall.

Matt joined him, feeling better now that he was being forced to stop thinking about Julie. It was more comfortable that way. It was what he was used to.

The barn door opened again.

Jeff and Justin charged into the barn.

Matt nodded in their direction but entered the stall with Dex.

Jeff blurted out, "Matt, I'm sorry the girls talked about Julie. They think it's for your own good."

Matt tensed again. "What are you talking about?"

"Dr. Lee convinced them you need to talk about Julie so you can get over her death," Jeff explained, his gaze anxious.

Righteous anger almost consumed Matt. So the doctor was the one who'd orchestrated the attack on his peace? Well, he'd make sure she understood he was not her patient!

He strode past the three men, his hands curled into fists, speaking to none of them.

"Matt, wait!" Jeff called.

He kept going.

"Way to go, Jeff," Justin said, his tones not congratulatory at all.

"Quit complaining and come on," Jeff called behind Matt. "We've got to stop him."

Chapter Five

In spite of Josie's threat, the ladies started to clean up as soon as all their eyes were dried of tears. They weren't fast, since the four pregnant women did everything at a slower speed these days, but they were getting the job done.

When the phone rang, Willie hustled over to answer. Then she turned to hand the phone to Elizabeth. "For you, Doctor."

With a frown, Elizabeth took the receiver. She'd left a message on her phone for anyone needing her to call the McIntyres' number. "Yes?"

"Dr. Lee, I think—" Barbie Ward broke off with a gasp.

"Barbie? What's wrong?"

"I…I think I'm in labor. I've been having a bad backache all day and…and my water broke an hour ago. The pain is getting worse."

Elizabeth kept her voice calm. "Yes, Barbie, I think you're in labor. How far apart are the contractions?"

"I don't know!" the woman wailed. "They're—coming pretty fast."

"Is your husband there with you?"

"Yes."

"Then ask him to drive you to the hospital. I'll meet you there." She almost hung up the phone, then put it back to her ear. "Barbie? Come straight to the hospital. Don't waste any time."

"Okay."

"Is it Barbie Ward?" Josie asked. "I didn't think she had a chance to win the contest. She's even bigger than us."

"Yes, it's her. She won't even make it to sunset today, much less New Year's. Sorry I have to run, Willie. Thank you for having me and— Oh! I don't have a car."

"Justin will drive you," Josie immediately volunteered.

Willie, however, had another plan. "Matt said he'd drive you if you had a call."

Elizabeth remembered Matt's less-than-happy exit. "Um, I hate to bother him. Maybe ''

The back door was thrown open and Matt stormed into the house. Anger stiffened his features, and his gaze honed in on Elizabeth, leaving no doubt about the target of his emotions.

"Dr. Lee—" he began with a roar.

Elizabeth wasn't afraid of him. She had more on her mind than Matt's feelings. Like getting things ready for Barbie. No one was at the hospital; in fact, it was an empty building most of the time, until it was needed. Elizabeth wished there could be a skeleton staff there ready for emergencies, but funding was scarce in a town the size of Bison City. Now she'd have to get her nurse, and probably Dave, there as soon as possible. And figure out how to care for the new mother and baby. But before she could get out the words to put Matt in his place, Willie intervened.

"You just hush up, Matt McIntyre, and go bring your truck around. Dr. Elizabeth has to get to the hospital. It's an emergency."

Matt stared at his housekeeper as if she'd spoken a foreign language.

Elizabeth turned to Jeff and Justin. "Could either of you take me to the hospital? You won't have to wait. I can get a ride home later."

Before they could respond, Matt whirled back around to stare at her. "I said I'd drive you if there was an emergency." Then he stomped back out of the house.

"Well, I guess that settles that," Josie said, staring after her brother.

Elizabeth realized Josie's words were accurate when the other two men shrugged their shoulders. She didn't have time to argue. "Annie, would you call Evelyn?" she asked, naming one of the two nurses in town. "She's on call today."

Then she hurried to grab her bag and coat and again thanked Willie for her hospitality. By the time she reached the back porch, Matt had his truck drawn up alongside and was getting out to help her in.

"I can manage," she called, clambering into the big truck with more speed than grace.

He slid back under the wheel, barely waiting for her to close her door before he hit the gas pedal.

"Who's the emergency?"

"Barbie Ward. I was afraid she might be a problem. She's got two little ones at home and tries to do more than she should."

With her mind on Barbie and what awaited her at the hospital, Elizabeth scarcely noticed the silence in the truck. In fact, she was grateful for it.

When the truck stopped, she quickly said, "Thanks. There's no need to wait. I'll get a ride home when it's over."

She didn't even realize that Matt had ignored her words until he reached out to hold the door open when she got it unlocked. "I said—"

"I heard you."

Well, fine, let him be stubborn again. She didn't have time to argue with him. She was the first to arrive, and there were preparations to be made.

As she gathered the supplies, Matt carried them into the procedure room. When another vehicle pulled up, he hurried out the door to offer his assistance. Within seconds Matt and Barbie's husband came in carrying Barbie.

Fortunately, Evelyn arrived right behind them.

Soon they had Barbie on the birthing table. Bill stood at his wife's head, clutching one of her hands. Elizabeth sent him a quick look, hoping the man didn't pass out. To her surprise she noted Matt standing beside him. Maybe Matt would catch him if he crashed.

"Is the baby going to be all right?" Barbie asked fearfully between pains. "It's early."

"I'm sure it will be, Barbie," Elizabeth said with a calm voice and a smile. "You're only a couple of weeks ahead of your due date." Elizabeth was concerned, but it wouldn't help to voice those concerns to Barbie now.

Elizabeth had already had Evelyn call Dave. She hated to interrupt his holiday, too, but since the baby could have problems, she thought he'd better be there.

He arrived just as the baby's head was crowning, coming to stand beside Elizabeth, a confident smile on his face.

"All right, Barbie, give one last big push, and we'll be celebrating your baby's birthday." Elizabeth smiled at the woman, then checked on her husband. Bill was sweating, clutching his wife's hand as if he were drowning.

"Bill, you okay?" she asked quickly.

"Yeah, sure. I'm here, Barbie," he whispered hoarsely.

When the baby slipped into Elizabeth's waiting hands, it gave a lusty yell without any prompting. A good sign.

"A boy, Barbie. You've got a son," Elizabeth announced. They already had two daughters. She knew Barbie had been hoping for a boy.

"Is he okay?" a teary-eyed Barbie asked faintly.

Dave wrapped the baby in a towel and took him

from Elizabeth so she could continue to help Barbie with the afterbirth. "He's just fine," he pronounced.

Barbie collapsed against the pillows…and her husband collapsed on top of her.

"Bill!" Elizabeth called, but before she or Evelyn could move, Matt grasped Bill's shoulders and hauled him off his wife.

"I'll take him to the waiting room," Matt assured them.

"Put his head between his knees," Elizabeth instructed, rolling her eyes.

He met her look with one of his own that told her he didn't need those instructions.

"Poor Bill," Barbie said, her breathing still heavy. "He did good, staying with me that long. The first time, before you moved here, he never made it past labor."

Dave had taken the baby into the other room to clean him up. Now he brought him back to his mom. "Here's your son, Barbie. After you take a gander at him, I'm going to put him in the incubator."

"Is something wrong?" Barbie asked, alarmed.

"Nope. We're just taking precautionary measures since he's early. He seems to be breathing pretty well."

Elizabeth felt as much relief as she was sure Barbie was feeling. Sometimes an early delivery was a miscalculation of when the conception occurred, but sometimes it was because of a problem with the baby. She wanted all her patients to have a happy ending.

She and Evelyn got Barbie settled in one of the three available beds in their little hospital. Though Barbie was tired after her efforts, she wasn't ready to go to sleep.

"Can you check on Bill?" she asked. "I'd like to see him."

"Sure," Elizabeth agreed. She could've sent Evelyn, but the nurse had more chores to do. Nodding in her direction, Elizabeth slipped into the waiting room.

Matt and Bill were sitting together, quietly talking. They both looked up, then rose.

Elizabeth, after one glance at Matt, turned to the other man. "Bill, Barbie is tucked in and wanting to see you."

"Great," he said, starting forward. Then he came to a halt. "Um, Dr. Lee, I'm sorry about…you know."

She smiled. "Yes, I know. That's all right. Go see Barbie, and maybe Dr. Dave will let you look in on your son."

He beamed at her and hurried away.

She turned to leave, unwilling to talk to Matt. She figured it might be best to ignore him until memories of the earlier events of the day had faded. The anger he'd worn on his face when he'd returned to the house hadn't been pleasant.

He didn't let her get away.

"Elizabeth."

With a sigh, she stopped and turned to face him.

"Yes?"

"Are you ready to go home?"

That was it? She considered his question, then opted for safety. "There's no need to concern yourself. Dave can drop me off later."

"I'll wait."

She frowned. Yes, he was definitely stubborn. "I have things to do."

"Doesn't matter. However long it takes, I'll wait. Then I'll take you home, and you and I are going to have a little discussion, Dr. Elizabeth Lee."

With a sigh, she nodded. There wasn't much point in delaying it. She should've known trying to help Matt McIntyre wouldn't be easy.

"I'll be back in a minute."

She returned to the procedure room and gave Evelyn some instructions, asking her to stay until she returned. She'd already decided to spend the night with Barbie. "Why don't you see if Alice can come in tomorrow. I'll take the nights. Then Saturday morning, maybe we'll be able to send Barbie home."

"You want me to stay tonight? You might not get much rest."

"I'll stay while I can," Elizabeth assured her. Patting her stomach, she added, "After I deliver, that may not be an option."

"I think we're going to need to enlist some new nurses. My sister works in Casper. I've been trying to get her to move. If she comes, will there be a job for her?"

Elizabeth nodded. "Yes, there will be. Dr. Dave

and I have been discussing our needs. Any way your sister could move now, before the Christmas rush?''

"Oh, she's already done most of her shopping—'' Evelyn broke off with a laugh. "You meant the rush of babies, didn't you? I'll call her. She might move that quickly.''

"Terrific. I'll be back as soon as I can.'' After she had her little discussion with Matt. She figured it would be brief. He'd yell, she'd quietly answer, he'd yell some more and storm out.

He was calmly waiting for her. She gave him a nod and walked to the outer door. He was there before her, holding it open.

After opening the passenger door of his truck, he slipped his hands under her arms and lifted her into the truck, as he had before. The man had perfect manners, if a woman liked being manhandled.

Or was very pregnant.

She settled back with a sigh. And that was the last sound in the cab of the truck until they stopped in front of her house.

"I guess I should ask you in," she said, easing into a smile. He might think they were going to fight, but she'd just had a good end to her day. A new baby made everything wonderful.

He cocked one eyebrow at her. "Yeah,'' he drawled and got out of the truck.

When she got her door open, he was there to help her to the ground. "Thanks.''

Without a word he closed the truck door and waited for her to precede him. He was really carrying this anger thing to the limit, maintaining his stoic silence.

She figured that silence was about to end.

Unlocking the door, she left it open for the silent man and headed for her favorite spot on the sofa, shrugging out of her coat as she went. "Do you want to have a seat, or are you going to tower over me while you read me the riot act?"

MATT DIDN'T WANT HER to look pretty, even when she was tired. Tucked behind her ears, her blond hair turned under, framing her delicate features. Her hazel eyes looked just the tiniest bit sleepy, like a child's at bedtime.

Damn it, she was an interfering busybody, destroying his peaceful life, and he wasn't going to have it. Just as he opened his mouth to make that idea clear to her, she spoke.

"Wasn't the baby beautiful? Barbie wanted a boy. They already have two girls, you know. Big brown eyes like their daddy and long blond pigtails like their mom. I wonder who the boy will look like." She closed her eyes, a smile playing on her soft lips.

She threw him off his stride. And reminded him of Julie and her happiness about her baby. "You're thinking of Sarah, aren't you?" he demanded, unable to help himself. "Who do you think she'll look like?"

Elizabeth smiled, not opening her eyes. "I don't know. Her daddy was blond, so I guess she'll be a blonde, but he had blue eyes. A blue-eyed blonde would be nice. But the most important thing is that she be healthy," she added with a sigh.

Matt frowned. "Is there anything wrong?"

Her eyes popped open. "No. But you just never know."

No. That was a lesson he'd learned well.

Which brought him full circle. "Listen, Elizabeth, Jeff said you told Josie to talk about Julie. We don't do that." That should be enough. She'd get the picture.

He was ready to stand and leave her alone, feeling he'd given her his warning. Not as harsh as he'd intended, but she looked tired. Enough said.

"Why?"

He stared at her, wondering if he'd heard correctly. "What did you say?"

With a gentle smile she said, "Why don't you talk about Julie?"

Anger filled him again. His emotions had been on a roller coaster today, all because of this woman. "That's my business!"

"I thought everyone loved her."

"Of course they did! She was perfect!" He realized he'd leaped to his feet and was yelling. But it was her fault.

"Was she, Matt? Was she perfect? I thought she was human. Humans are never perfect."

"Don't you dare say anything bad about Julie!"

She reached out and took his hand. "Matt, I'm not trying to criticize Julie. It's you I'm criticizing. You're not letting her live."

"Damn it, don't you understand anything? Julie's dead!'' He wanted to run, to escape the torture she was putting him through. But he stood frozen to the ground.

Suddenly Elizabeth was standing beside him, her arms holding him.

''Matt, I know she's dead,'' she whispered, her voice velvet soft, ''and you can't bring her back. But she can live in your heart, in your memory. She can live in the family's memory, if you talk about her. Her spirit can embrace you, even let you forgive yourself, if you'll stop hiding her away in the dark.''

He couldn't speak. But he held on to the woman pressed against him for all he was worth. At least she was warm and alive; at the moment he wasn't so sure about himself.

Her hands stroked his back, beneath his leather jacket, soothing him, encouraging him, though he wasn't sure what he was supposed to do. His world seemed to have collided with some unrecognizable force and knocked him off center.

How long he stood there holding Elizabeth against him, he couldn't say. Whether he would have released her anytime in the near future, he didn't know. But when her baby kicked against him, he dropped his arms and quickly stepped away.

''It's only Sarah,'' she said softly.

He ground his teeth together and, barely moving his lips, said, ''Listen to me. I am not your patient. Stop messing with my world. I like it the way it is!''

Then he escaped from Elizabeth Lee's softness. A softness that he couldn't be around. She was making him soft. And he had to remain strong. He had to take charge, to care for his family, to provide. He had to get out of there.

ELIZABETH FELL BACK onto the sofa.

She needed to gather some things together to go back to the hospital, but she had to have a minute. Holding Matt in her arms was an incredible experience.

"Quit acting like a teenager!" she muttered. But he was an attractive man. She wasn't interested, of course. Dale had been her best friend. The idea of being together the rest of their lives, of raising a family together, had made the future look good. Predictable. Comfortable.

But it was different with Matt. Holding him disturbed her. Made her antsy. Left her wanting something.

It must be that famous hormonal imbalance she warned her patients about. She'd had teary moments the past seven months, but she hadn't experienced a surge of sexual hunger.

Until now.

She sighed again. It didn't matter. Matt would never know, and she wouldn't touch him again. If she was right, she wouldn't have to. Tonight, that fortress he'd put up around his heart had cracked open.

Or at least she thought it had. Change wouldn't

happen overnight, but she didn't think even Matt could crawl back in his hole.

Maybe she should encourage Josie to start looking for a lady for Matt. Someone who could bake a cherry pie. And make quilts. A woman who would devote her entire life to a good man.

There was that cute waitress at Nell's.

Maybe the new hotel clerk at The Way Station, Jeff's hotel. She'd ask Bailey.

Or maybe Annie knew of someone.

Willie had her ear to the ground in Bison City. She'd know if there were any single women.

With all the women in the McIntyre family, they didn't need her help in finding a woman for Matt. In no time he'd have a new wife, and she'd have a new patient, eager to extend the McIntyre line.

She'd call them tomorrow. She'd celebrate tomorrow, too. Darn it, she'd even smile tomorrow.

But not tonight. She had work to do.

Chapter Six

Matt didn't go straight home.

Without conscious decision, he drove to the small cemetery on the ranch where the McIntyres buried their own. Samuel and Jocasta, the original Wyoming McIntyres, were buried there, along with each successive generation.

The only recent graves were those of Julie and their baby. They'd been laid to rest side by side in one corner near a stand of aspens.

Matt hadn't visited their graves. It was because he refused to dwell on their deaths, he assured himself. But according to Elizabeth, it was because he was shutting them away. Had he done that? Had he lost them because he hadn't mentally taken out his memories and breathed life into them?

Instead of getting out of the truck, Matt sat behind the wheel, staring through the glass at the two monuments he'd had placed on their graves. Julie and their son, Thomas Samuel McIntyre. Matt had been in so much pain. Wanted to die himself, to join Julie and little Thomas in oblivion.

"Damn it," he exclaimed, pounding a fist on the steering wheel, "it hurt too bad."

Had he gone too far? Shut out his memories to erase his pain? Isolated himself in his work because the cows didn't make demands on him?

He'd had work to do. His parents had stayed a couple of weeks after the funeral. Then he'd sent them back to Florida, to the life they'd built there. Their tiptoeing around him only reminded him of his loss. It was easier when only he and Willie lived in the big house meant for big families.

Hiding again.

Finally he started his truck and headed for that house.

Earlier today it had been full of family and friends. He'd been the one to wreck the holiday meal. It was cowardly to hope they would've all gone home. It was after six, but it was tradition to watch football all afternoon and then have leftovers for dinner.

Tradition had held.

When he opened the kitchen door, eight faces turned to stare at him. Then Willie spoke. "Well, get on in here. We saved you some turkey. How's Barbie?"

Matt did as Willie ordered, but he avoided all the stares. Tossing his hat onto a peg near the door, he shrugged out of his coat and hung it up. Then he joined the others.

"She's better than Bill. He's the one who passed out."

Justin paled. "He did? It was that bad?"

Matt noted the worried looks on the three pregnant ladies, Josie, Annie and Bailey. He could almost hear Elizabeth's soothing, calm voice every time she'd spoken to Barbie. "Naw. He's just a weenie." He smiled at the ladies, glad to see the relief on their faces. "And thcy had a boy," he added, though his voice cracked a little on the last word.

"Girls are just as good," Bailey said, raising her chin, amid the congratulations. Her doctor in New York had told her she was having a girl.

Jeff's arm encircled her shoulders. "They're a lot prettier."

"No argument here," Matt agreed with a smile. He thought of Elizabeth's description of Sarah. He figured the kid would have to be beautiful with Elizabeth for a mother.

Josie finally spoke. "Matt, did you— I mean, are you still mad at Elizabeth? And us?"

He wasn't ready for an examination of his emotions, but he didn't want Josie upset. "No." Then he turned his attention to the leftovers. Suddenly he was hungry.

Hours later, when everyone had gone home, he wandered back into the kitchen, looking for a snack.

Willie was sitting at the table, working a crossword puzzle, one of her favorite pastimes. "Need something?"

"I thought I might have another piece of Bailey's cake. She's sure a good baker."

"Yep, a good addition to this family. I'm glad she and Jeff have decided to marry."

"Me, too. When we talked to Mom and Dad earlier, they were pleased, too."

Willie seemed to realize he was thinking of his youngest brother who was missing. "Give Alex time, Matt. He'll come around."

He looked at her sharply. "Do you think so?"

"He always has. He's a McIntyre."

"Annie hasn't said it's Alex's baby."

Willie chuckled. "He's the only man she's ever looked at. And I can count. Josie got pregnant right after her wedding. Bailey was at the wedding and gone after the weekend. Annie's due at the same time as both of them."

"The last time Alex was home," Matt muttered. "You're right, Willie, it's got to be his baby."

"Yep. By the way, there's some of that cherry pie left in the refrigerator." She kept her gaze on the crossword puzzle.

Matt's hand froze on the cake lid. He loved cherry pie, but he'd shoved away his piece of pie earlier because Elizabeth had admitted she'd bought it from Nell. He'd placed too much importance on her making it herself.

After another glance at Willie's averted face, he opened the refrigerator door and took out the lone slice. "Looks like everybody wanted some."

"Yep. But I saved you a piece."

He grabbed a fork and carried it to the table. "Thanks. Nell's pies are always good."

"It was nice of Dr. Elizabeth to bring it."

Matt stiffened. "I thought you'd be on my side, Willie. Everyone else cooked whatever they brought."

"And how many of them delivered a baby?"

"None of them," he snapped, frowning.

"So, we all have different talents."

Matt wasn't going down without a fight. "You should see her refrigerator! There's nothing in it. How's she going to take care of a child?"

"She'll find a way," Willie said calmly. "And I'll add her to my list."

"What list?"

"I take food to Annie on Thursdays, to make sure she gets a good meal every now and again. I'll do the same for Dr. Elizabeth. It's hard to get enthusiastic about cooking when you're pregnant and alone."

Matt sent her a gentle smile. "You're a good woman, Wilhemena."

"And you're a good man, Matt McIntyre, but that don't mean you aren't sometimes wrong. Now eat your pie and get to bed. The sun'll be up early tomorrow."

She left him no opportunity to answer, leaving the room, carrying her crossword puzzle with her.

ELIZABETH DIDN'T GET much sleep that night. The newborn needed checking every two hours. By morning her eyes were gritty from lack of sleep.

When Alice arrived, she hurriedly headed for home. There were no patients scheduled for the day, and she needed sleep.

But first she stopped off at Nell's Chuck Wagon Café for a much-needed breakfast.

"Dr. Elizabeth!" Nell exclaimed, surprised to see her. "I hear Bison City got a new citizen last night."

Elizabeth smiled. "Mother and baby are doing fine. But I need some sleep. I spent the night at the hospital."

"You shouldn't be doin' that in your condition. Come sit down. What'll you have?"

"Mmm, a stack of your famous buttermilk pancakes and a big glass of milk," Elizabeth ordered. When Nell hurried into the kitchen, Elizabeth closed her eyes and took a deep sniff of the coffee aroma that always filled the restaurant in the mornings.

She missed her cup of coffee.

"What are you doing here?" a deep voice growled, and her eyes popped open. She hadn't expected to see Matt McIntyre for a week or two. Even then, she wasn't sure he'd be willing to speak to her.

"I'm having breakfast."

"You got out of bed at this time of the morning just to have Nell cook you breakfast?"

His scorn stung.

"No."

"I bought you some cereal. Wouldn't that have been better than dressing and coming up here?" He acted like he hadn't heard her answer.

"I haven't been to bed, and I was already

dressed,'' she snapped, irritation chasing away her serenity.

Without asking, Matt slid into the other side of the booth and put his Stetson on the windowsill. ''What do you mean you haven't been to bed? Did you deliver another baby last night?''

''No,'' she said with a sigh. Did everyone have to have answers about her life? ''I stayed at the hospital last night with Barbie and her baby. It was a busy night.''

''She and the baby are okay, aren't they?'' He leaned toward her. ''I mean, I took a present by a few minutes ago, but I didn't even ask. I just assumed—''

''Matt, they're fine. But newborns need a lot of attention. They don't sleep all that long at first.''

''Oh. I wouldn't know.''

Before she could say anything, Nell arrived at the table with a glass of milk. ''Mornin', cowboy. Want some coffee?''

''Yes, please,'' Matt said, accepting her offer with a smile. Then he frowned at Elizabeth. ''Unless the smell of it makes you sick?''

She shook her head. ''No. I may turn green with envy, but it won't make me sick.''

''You can't drink it?''

''It's not good for expectant mothers,'' Nell assured him firmly before Elizabeth could say anything. ''They need to be drinkin' milk.'' She grabbed a cup and saucer and returned to the table with a pot of fresh coffee. ''Here you go, Matt.''

''Thanks.''

After Nell walked away, Matt sipped his coffee, keeping his head down. Then, to Elizabeth's surprise, he said, "Julie threw up every time she smelled coffee. I started going to the bunkhouse in the mornings so I could have a cup."

"That was thoughtful of you." When he raised his head to look at her, she rewarded him with a smile.

"I hadn't thought about that since…since she died."

"Tragedy has a way of wiping out some memories."

"How do you know?"

She knew he wasn't asking about her last remark. "A combination of things. My training. Experience with patients. Learning to read people. And having gone through a tragedy myself."

"I dreamed of her last night."

She studied his face, looking for signs of lack of sleep, but she didn't see any. All she saw was a strong, handsome man. "Are you all right?"

He grimaced. "Yeah, I'm not going to fall apart on you the way I did last night."

She sensed his embarrassment even if his words hadn't indicated it. "If you think that's falling apart, mister, you've got a lot to learn." With a broad smile, she launched into some descriptions of patients', or their husbands', embarrassing moments that brought a few smiles to Matt's face. Which made him all the more attractive.

Nell arrived back at their table with two plates full of pancakes.

Elizabeth was surprised. "I didn't know you ordered pancakes," she said to Matt.

"I don't have to order 'em. Nell knows what I want."

"I'm thinking you're one spoiled cowboy," she teased, "what with all the ladies in town looking out for you."

"Just Nell and Willie," he assured her.

"There are a few others who would apply for the job," Nell inserted, "but he don't encourage them."

"Maybe it's time he did," Elizabeth said, grinning. "You know, he needs to have someone in training before either of you gets too old to slave over a hot stove all day."

"Good idea," Nell agreed, smiling at Matt. "I'll start lookin' around for a likely candidate." Then she hurried back to the kitchen.

"Thanks a lot, Elizabeth," Matt drawled. "That's all I need, for half the female population in Bison City to be after me."

"Half? You're not very conceited, are you?" she teased, though she figured it would be closer to 100 percent of the single women, who'd be on his trail.

"Matt! Elizabeth!" Jeff called as he and Bailey stepped into the café. "What are you two doing here? I mean—"

Bailey elbowed him in the side. "Nice to see both of you. May we join you?"

Matt cocked an eyebrow at Elizabeth. She nodded and smiled at the new arrivals.

Standing, Matt shoved his plate of pancakes

across the table, then slid in beside Elizabeth. As she realized his intention, she hurriedly slid over, but not before his long length was pressed against hers.

"If you get yourself a coffee cup, Jeff, I've already got a pot here on the table." He looked at Bailey. "None for you."

"My doctor—" she nodded at Elizabeth "—says I can have a cup if I desperately need it, but Nell won't hear of such a thing."

"She'll bring you some milk," Elizabeth said, smiling in sympathy.

Which, of course, Nell did, along with more pancakes.

"Are you all right, Elizabeth? You look tired," Bailey commented.

With a sigh Elizabeth explained her night's work.

"How often do babies wake up at first?" Jeff asked with a frown.

"It varies. Some babies need to be fed every two hours, others can make it three hours."

Jeff looked taken aback. "But how does the mother ever get any rest?"

Elizabeth smiled. "If she's lucky, the daddy gives her some relief."

"But he can't— I mean, if she's nursing, how can he—" Jeff turned bright red.

Bailey shook her head and rolled her eyes. "Can you believe he's embarrassed by discussing breast feeding?"

"He'll get used to it," Elizabeth assured her. "Jeff, a woman can express some of her breast milk and store it in the fridge. Or sometimes we can supplement her milk with formula. It all depends on the circumstances.''

''Oh. Thanks for explaining.'' Jeff stabbed his pancakes.

''What?'' Bailey demanded.

He turned to look at her. ''I didn't say anything.''

''No, but I can hear you thinking.''

Matt nudged Elizabeth. They exchanged a smile that gave her a warm feeling. It was like sharing a moment with a friend. Then he leaned forward. ''If you can hear this guy thinking, Bailey, you're worse off than I thought.''

She blushed, and they all laughed.

Then Matt asked, ''What are you two doing here when you've got an entire restaurant kitchen at your command?''

Jeff squeezed Bailey's shoulders. ''We walk to breakfast occasionally so Bailey gets some exercise. We usually go to the Silver Horn Grill because it's farther away, but we were too hungry today. Her doctor recommended exercise.''

Matt stared at the diminishing stack of pancakes. ''Those kind of defeat the purpose, don't they?''

''I didn't recommend exercise for Bailey to lose weight,'' Elizabeth explained. ''She's at the perfect weight. But the exercise keeps her healthy. It may even shorten her labor time.''

Matt stared at her. ''I didn't know that. Do you exercise?''

''I try to use the treadmill at the hospital three

times a week," she said, ignoring the warmth that again filled her at his expression of concern.

She'd been alone for the past six months, having to be strong for her patients and strong for herself. Everyone assumed she had no problems because she was a doctor. But it touched her that Matt cared.

Jeff immediately asked, "Should I get a treadmill for the inn? So Bailey can use it afterward?"

Bailey groaned. "Let's not worry about afterward until I've had this child. Noelle will be enough to deal with at first."

"You've named your baby, too?" Matt asked.

"Too? Have the others named their babies?" Bailey asked.

"I don't know, but Elizabeth— It's not a secret, is it?" he asked, looking at her.

"No, of course not. I've named my baby Sarah Elizabeth," she explained to the other two.

"Oh, that's a pretty name. You can call her Sarah Beth, if you want," Bailey exclaimed. "I told you I'm having a girl, too. I call her Noelle because she's due around Christmas." Bailey cast a look at Matt. "You probably think it's silly to name her already, but—"

"No," he said abruptly. "It's not silly. Julie and I named our baby as soon as we found out he was a boy. Thomas Samuel. That was his name."

Jeff and Bailey stared at Matt, and Elizabeth could feel his embarrassment. "Are those family names?" she asked casually, taking another bite of pancake.

It was Jeff who answered. "Samuel is. Our great-

great-great—or is it only two greats? I get confused. Anyway, Samuel McIntyre settled here a long time ago with his wife Jocasta. That's who Josie is named after.''

''What a wonderful heritage,'' Elizabeth commented.

''Yeah,'' Matt agreed with a grin, his embarrassment forgotten. ''We've teased Josie about it a lot because Grandfather Samuel and Jocasta were in a shipwreck. He had a couple of bags of gold he intended to bring ashore, but he had to drop them to save Jocasta,'' Matt explained. ''We told Josie that any man would choose the gold over her, so she'd better be glad she doesn't live near an ocean.''

''Matt!'' Elizabeth and Bailey protested simultaneously.

''I heard that, Matt McIntyre!'' Josie exclaimed over his shoulder.

Matt turned around to find Justin and Josie standing there. ''Damn! What is this, a family reunion? We only need Alex and Annie to make it complete.''

''*We* are taking a coffee break after already working several hours,'' Josie righteously informed him. ''I don't know why the rest of you are lolling around, wasting away the day.''

There was a lot of protest from the men of the group. Matt explained about Elizabeth's night of work, too, saving her the trouble of answering any questions.

Jeff suggested, ''Let's move to the big booth in the back. Then we can visit.''

As they all began to gather dishes to move, Elizabeth said, "I can't stay, but you go ahead. I really have to get some sleep."

Matt set his plate and cup back on the table. "You're going home now?"

"Yes," she said with a smile, albeit a tired one.

"I'd better follow you home," he said, sliding out of the booth and extending his hand to her.

She stared at him, thinking she must've misheard him. "What?"

"I'll follow you home, make sure you get there all right. Or maybe you'd better leave your car here. You can walk up later and get it. That way you'll get in some exercise, too."

"Well, thanks for planning my day, but I don't think so," Elizabeth said, hoping he caught the sarcasm.

"Why not?"

"Because I might have an emergency call. I wouldn't have time to walk up here to get my car." She ignored his extended hand and scooted to the edge of the booth.

Matt took her arm, since she hadn't accepted his hand, and pulled her up. In truth, she was grateful for his help, because her tiredness was making her weak. But that didn't mean she was going to tell him that.

"Leave your keys here," Jeff said. "I can drop Bailey off at the inn, when we leave, and drive your car to your house and walk back to the inn."

"That's not necessary," Elizabeth began.

"Thanks, Jeff. That's a good plan. Give him your

keys, Elizabeth,'' Matt ordered, as if he were in control.

"You are not my boss, Matt McIntyre,'' she protested, but the ferocity of her words was undermined by a huge yawn.

"See? It wouldn't be safe for you to drive,'' Matt assured her. "Don't be stubborn. Give Jeff your keys.''

He was calling *her* stubborn? Expelling a puff of breath that came out more as a sigh than exasperation, she dug into her purse and did as he'd said.

"Thank you, Jeff. I appreciate it.''

"No problem. Get yourself some rest. I'll put the keys in your mailbox.''

With a smile only mildly triumphant, Matt guided her to the door, adding to Josie and Justin, "Now there's no need to move. You can have our places.''

"Got everything arranged to your satisfaction?'' she muttered as they exited the café. "I swear, you'd think the entire town couldn't function without your guidance.''

"I'm not concerned about the town. Just the McIntyres,'' he assured her, still grinning.

"I'm not a McIntyre!''

"But you're important to the McIntyres. You're going to be delivering three McIntyre babies in the near future. That fact makes you real important to us.''

Of course. She wasn't important to Matt McIntyre except for delivering his nieces or nephews.

She needed to remember that.

BACK IN THE CAFÉ, the four watched Matt and Elizabeth through the window.

"What's going on?" Bailey asked. "Are they—"

"I don't know," Josie said breathlessly, "but wouldn't it be wonderful?"

"What are you two talking about?" Justin asked.

Josie rolled her eyes. "We're talking about them being a couple, you dufus."

"Hey, don't call me names," Justin protested, grinning.

"Do you think that's a good idea?" Jeff asked.

"Why not?" Bailey wanted to know, staring at him.

"Well, he lost his wife and baby. Maybe he— I mean, he might confuse what he feels for the doctor with the need to—you know, replace Julie and the baby."

Both women protested, but Josie frowned. She didn't want to think Jeff might be right, but he could be. She'd have to sound out Elizabeth.

She just wanted her brother to be happy again.

Chapter Seven

Matt returned to the ranch after escorting Elizabeth home. He had work to do.

But he was amazed at how much easier those chores looked than they had in the past. Some days it had felt as if his boots were mired in molasses when he tried to do his job. And his heart had definitely weighed him down.

Could it be true? Could remembering Julie and baby Thomas make such a difference? Remembering the good times, the nights he held Julie in his arms, feeling the baby move inside her, sharing their hopes and plans for the future?

There was still some pain. Probably there always would be, but it wasn't as raw as before. And maybe, with time, it would grow even less.

After working all day, he reached the house at sunset, his bones weary and his flesh cold. The winds had penetrated his jeans and even his jacket at times.

''Where's the coffee, Willie?'' he called as he came in the back door.

"Same place as usual," she returned. The table was already set for the two of them, fragrant smells filling the kitchen.

He grinned and grabbed a mug. "Good. I don't know what I'd do without you."

She cocked an eyebrow at him. "You're in an awful good mood, Matt McIntyre. What's going on?"

"Had a good day's work."

"So? You've had them before. You'd think you'd found old Samuel's bags of gold." She put several dishes on the table and gestured for Matt to sit down.

As he did so, after washing his hands at the sink, he said, "You know the gold wasn't what made Samuel happy."

"Humph! I'm not sure there are too many men like Samuel who'd choose a woman over bags of gold. Especially today."

Matt filled his plate. "Maybe not. But they're the losers. Look at Jeff and Bailey. Do you think he'd trade her for gold?"

"I hope not. They've got a little one to take care of."

"Yeah, I hope Alex realizes—"

"I told you he would. In fact, I'm bettin' he and Annie are married soon, too."

"I might take you up on that bet, just to lose."

"'Course," Willie continued, as if he hadn't spoken, "you'd be the only McIntyre bachelor left if that happened. It would be open season on Matt McIntyre."

"Hey!" Matt protested, almost choking since he'd just taken a big bite of mashed potatoes. After swallowing, he stared at Willie. "That's not funny."

"Wasn't meant to be. It's serious business, taking a wife."

"But I'm not—" Matt stopped as a picture of Elizabeth filled his mind. He shook his head. She wasn't wife material. Certainly not a rancher's wife. He'd need someone like Julie if he ever— When had marriage become a possibility for him?

Because he'd just realized it was.

"What's the matter? Cat got your tongue?" Willie asked, watching him.

"No. I was concentrating on my supper, Willie. You outdid yourself tonight."

"It's a casserole, Matt," his housekeeper pointed out, her eyebrows raised. "Hamburger and noodles and a few vegetables thrown in."

"But it's really good. And healthy. Maybe I should take some to Annie and, uh, Dr. Elizabeth," he added casually, hoping Willie wouldn't comment on his list.

Though she stared at him, she only said, "There's plenty."

"Good. I'll do that as soon as I've finished." And had a shower. He wouldn't want to go calling on the ladies smelling like a horse. Though Annie wouldn't mind, he admitted with a grin. Elizabeth might.

He rose as soon as he'd hurriedly eaten. "You

call both of them and tell them I'm coming. I'll go clean up a little.''

Willie fixed two dishes of the casserole, stopping when she heard the shower turn on upstairs. Matt was showering before delivering the food? She smiled.

Yeah, he was the humanitarian-type tonight. She'd bet he wore his favorite blue shirt, too, the one that made his eyes to-die-for.

MATT WORRIED all the way into town. Annie, according to Willie, had sounded grateful for the casserole. She'd helped her uncle Dex at the animal hospital because they'd had a couple of emergencies. She'd just gotten home when Willie had called.

Elizabeth hadn't answered her phone.

Making a quick stop at Annie's, he asked her, casual-like, if she knew where Elizabeth might be. ''Willie fixed a dish for her, too, and I'd hate for it to go to waste.''

''She's probably at the hospital. You know, taking care of Barbie and the baby.''

''Damn, she spent last night there. The woman needs her rest.'' He turned and headed for the door, his thoughts all centered on Elizabeth.

''Matt?'' Annie called. ''Thanks for the food. And Elizabeth is very good at her job. She'll be all right.''

''Yeah.''

Didn't Annie realize that Elizabeth couldn't cut back, like Annie had? She didn't have an Uncle

Dex waiting in the wings to replace her. Dave Gardner, the other doctor, already had a full caseload. And his wife was expecting, too, though she wasn't due until March.

He pulled into the hospital parking lot, seeing Elizabeth's small car parked in lonely splendor. She really needed to get a truck of some kind, an SUV that could handle Wyoming winters. He'd talk to her about that.

When he entered the hospital, the reception room was empty, but he could hear soft, womanly voices in the distance.

"Elizabeth?" he called as he moved to the open doorway.

She appeared quickly. "Matt! What are you doing here? Is something wrong?"

"No. I tried to call you, but you didn't answer."

"Well, no, because I'm here. What did you need?"

He held out the casserole dish. "Willie wanted you to have some supper."

"How did she know—how thoughtful of her. Barbie and I were just discussing calling Nell's to see if she'd deliver some dinner for us." She took the casserole from his hands with a smile.

A dismissing smile.

Matt remained firmly in place. He wasn't going anywhere. "I'll visit with you while you eat. Then I can take the empty dish back to Willie."

"That's not necessary, Matt. I'll wash it before I return it. You can tell Willie I won't lose it." Again she smiled at him.

"Is Barbie up to a visit? How's the baby?"

She seemed surprised. "I'll ask her."

Matt waited for her return. He wasn't sure why he was so intent on not leaving. Maybe it was the paperwork he had waiting for him at home. He hated paperwork.

Elizabeth reappeared. "Barbie says to come on back. She wants to thank you for the casserole, too."

He followed Elizabeth down the small hall, watching her graceful walk. From the back, it wasn't apparent she was pregnant, and he recognized a flare of sexual interest that he immediately tried to squelch.

"Here he is, Barbie, our dinner provider," Elizabeth announced as they entered the small hospital room.

"Thank you so much, Matt. It was so thoughtful of Willie to think of me," Barbie said, as if she had been the intent of Willie's gesture.

"No problem. You know how Willie tries to take care of everyone." He was surprised to discover the baby sleeping in one corner of the room. "The baby's in here?" he asked.

"Sure," Barbie said with a big smile. "I don't like to let him out of my sight."

Matt couldn't resist. He stepped over to the side of the bassinet. The old pain that had filled him whenever he saw a little boy and thought of his own child was there, but not as bad. With a shaking hand, he ran one finger over the tiny fist.

"He's so little," he whispered.

Suddenly Elizabeth was beside him, her hand touching his arm. "Don't you believe it. He weighed almost six pounds. He's a big boy, for one who came a couple of weeks early."

She knew. He stared down into her eyes and saw sympathy there, understanding. The urge to kiss her soft lips, to thank her for being there, rattled him. What was he thinking?

He moved back and cleared his throat. "You two had better eat before it gets cold."

"I think we have some plates and a few pieces of odd silverware in the storage closet," Elizabeth murmured, moving away from him.

"What will you drink?"

"We'll get something out of the soda machine, if I can find the right change," Elizabeth muttered from behind the opened door of the closet.

"I'll get them," he muttered, and hurried back down the hall. The soda machine in the waiting room was one of the ways they raised money for the hospital.

The Millennium Baby Contest was going to do a better job of funding the improvements. A much better job. But every little bit helped.

He got three drinks from the machine. He didn't really want one, but he figured Elizabeth wouldn't kick him out if he bought himself something to drink, too.

When he got back to Barbie's room, he discovered her sitting up in bed, tasting the casserole. Elizabeth was just sitting down in a nearby chair, but she straightened as Matt entered.

"Thanks, Matt. You shouldn't have—"

"Sit down. Did you get any sleep today?"

His abrupt question distracted her as she sat down. "Yes, of course I did."

"Who's taking the night shift tonight?" That question had bothered him as soon as he heard Elizabeth was at the hospital again.

Barbie turned startled eyes on him. Elizabeth ignored his stare. "I am, of course. The nurses are needed during the day, to help Dave."

"Damn it, Elizabeth! You can't keep doing this. It's too much for a pregnant woman."

Barbie chimed in. "Oh, Dr. Elizabeth, I didn't think! I could've asked one of my friends to stay. I'm so sorry!" she exclaimed, tears filling her eyes.

Elizabeth glared at Matt, then turned calmly to her patient. "Don't be silly, Barbie. This is my job, and I'm darned good at it, if I do say so myself. Now, eat your dinner while I have a chat with Mr. McIntyre."

She pulled herself up from the chair, set her plate on the seat. Then she grabbed Matt's arm and pulled him from the room.

Once she had him on the other side of the closed door, she let him have it. "Matt McIntyre, don't you ever upset one of my patients again! How could you be so thoughtless? She's at a very vulnerable point. The exhilaration has worn off and she needs to be reassured, not worried."

"But what about you?" he argued, irritated by her reprimand. "Who's going to take care of you?"

Exasperated, she sighed, then looked at him

again, her hazel eyes widening. "Matt, I'm not your daughter, your wife or your sister. *And* I'm an adult trained to do my job. Most important of all, I love my baby and would never do anything to harm her. You have to trust me."

Surprisingly, he found he did. She would ask more of herself than she should. But he believed her.

"Okay, I'm sorry. Now will you go back and finish your meal?" He needed her to move away from him before he swept her into a bear hug. Or kissed her.

"Yes, of course. Thanks for coming by." Then she walked back into Barbie's room as if she thought he was leaving.

Wrong.

"Is everything okay?" Barbie asked anxiously.

"Of course it is," Elizabeth returned. "Matt is overprotective, you know. It comes from being a little spoiled."

"Oh, yeah?" Matt growled, but his lips curved in amusement as Elizabeth jumped. "I reckon I'm going to keep you company for a while, Barbie, so the good doctor won't bad-mouth me."

Barbie relaxed in the bed and smiled at him. "Good idea. There's no telling what she'd say if you left."

"Right. Is Bill coming to see you tonight?"

"Oh, yes," Barbie replied, a glow on her face. "He called a little while ago. He's getting the girls dressed. They're going to see their brother for the first time."

Matt's gaze flew to Elizabeth as he dealt with the ache in his heart of what might have been. But there was also a hunger to experience those joys himself, a hunger that he hadn't admitted to himself before tonight. A hunger that had something to do with Elizabeth.

"It will be a real special occasion," he said softly, his gaze going back to the new mother.

"Yes. I can't wait— Oh! He's awake, Dr. Elizabeth," Barbie said, putting her plate on the bed tray.

Matt leaped to his feet, setting his soda on a shelf and moving to the bassinet. "Has he got his eyes open?"

A mewly cry came from the tiny infant. Matt's fingers itched to pick the baby up and he looked over his shoulder at Elizabeth.

She was calmly eating her dinner.

"Elizabeth, aren't you going to do something?"

Grinning, she said, "It's not necessary. Both of you are eager to do whatever you can. But you really should wait until he lets out a good cry. Let him exercise his lungs."

"But he's awake," Matt protested, his gaze returning to the baby. What a miracle, he thought, a baby who survived, who lived and breathed, who cried.

As if on cue, the whimper became a lusty wail.

"He's hungry," Barbie assured him eagerly.

Matt understood her enthusiasm. Hunger was a good sign, a sign of life, of growth—like the hunger he'd experienced earlier.

That thought stopped him. And reassured him. Yes, he was alive. Maybe it was about damn time he realized it.

"Shall I feed him, Dr. Elizabeth?" Barbie asked.

"Sounds like he's ready for it," Elizabeth agreed. She set down her now-empty plate. "Matt, you might want to wait outside, while Barbie feeds the baby."

"No, I want—" Then he realized what Elizabeth meant. Barbie was going to breastfeed. "Oh, of course. But, Barbie, can I hang around and see the baby after you've fed him?"

"Of course you can, Matt. I'll even let you hold him."

With that promise, Matt headed for the waiting room.

ELIZABETH WATCHED HIM GO. He was going to be all right. She'd realized it when he reached out to touch the baby. Now he wanted to hold him.

"That was sweet of you, Barbie, offering to let Matt hold the baby."

Barbie smiled. "Matt's a good man. We all hated what he went through. Don't you think it's a good sign that he wants to?"

"I do, indeed. Now, let's get this child fed so he'll stop screaming at us." She lifted the baby and handed him to his mother.

A few minutes later she stepped to the door of the waiting room to discover Matt staring out the window, his hands on his hips.

"Matt?"

He spun around, a fierce look on his face.

"Are you all right?"

"Yeah, sure. Is she finished?"

"She is. The baby is waiting for you to hold him."

She was glad they weren't in a race, because Matt's long strides ate up the distance to the other room. By the time she reached the door, he was standing by Barbie.

"Here you go, Matt. Just be careful," Barbie warned, her motherly instincts adding the caution.

Suddenly Matt looked unsure of himself. "Uh, what if I drop him?"

Barbie squeaked in fear, but Elizabeth laughed. "Don't be silly, Matt. Your hands are bigger than he is." But she saw the real panic in his face and added, "If you want, you can sit down and I'll hand him to you."

"Yeah, okay."

Once the transfer was made, she stepped back and was surprised by the sudden tears that filled her eyes. The look on Matt's face was one of awe.

"You want to look at him?" she asked. Without waiting for an answer, she moved back to his side and unwrapped the baby as he held him. The cooler air caused the baby to squirm and protest.

"I don't think he likes that," he said softly, his gaze never leaving the tiny infant.

"No, he likes being wrapped up snugly. After all, he's been in tight quarters for nine months." She rubbed her own protruding stomach as she spoke. Matt's gaze lifted and followed her hand.

"Sarah Beth protesting? Maybe she's jealous," he said, a teasing smile on his face that made her want to touch him.

She cleared her throat. "Probably."

The sound of the front door opening aroused Barbie. "Oh! I think my family's here."

Elizabeth knew she'd want her baby in her arms. She took the little boy from Matt, wrapping him back up expertly, and handed him to his mother.

"Matt, why don't you go tell Bill it's okay to come on back," she suggested.

He rose, but before he did as she asked, he touched Barbie's hand. "Thanks, Barbie." Then he hurried out of the room.

Both ladies' eyes were misty as they looked at each other.

"He's a good man," Barbie repeated.

Elizabeth nodded. "Just like your man. I'll go keep Matt company while you visit. Let me know if you need anything."

Once Bill and the two little girls went in to see Barbie and the baby, the waiting room seemed very silent.

Matt was again staring out the window.

She approached him and put her hand on his arm. "Are you okay?"

"Yeah, sure."

That seemed to be his standard answer, but she suspected the evening had been difficult for him. "Babies are sweet, aren't they?"

"Babies are miracles," he whispered, not looking at her.

"I know. That's why I love my work."

His hand covered hers where it rested on his arm, and he turned to look at her. "I've birthed a lot of calves and foals, but I'd never seen a human birth until Barbie's. It's amazing."

"Yes," she agreed with a smile.

"What did they name him? I forgot to ask."

"James Allen Ward."

Matt smiled. "It suits him. Isn't it amazing how he already has a personality? I mean, I thought babies were kind of generic. All alike, but—"

"Matt, you're right, but you haven't been around all that many babies. Wait until after Christmas. Then you'll really be an expert."

"Yeah," he agreed with a chuckle, but she was pleased with the satisfaction that filled that one syllable.

"Do you think Sarah Beth will like her name?"

His question surprised her. "I hope so. But sometimes, as they grow older, they wish they had something exotic like Jewel or whatever is popular."

"Will she be as big as James Allen?"

Elizabeth shrugged. "I'm guessing she'll be a little bigger, unless she comes early, too, but it's hard to tell. A lot depends on when she arrives."

"You've got everything ready?"

With a sigh, she confessed, "No. Not yet. I'm going to go into town soon and buy what I'll need, but...but I've been busy. I'll get it all done in time."

She tried to smile, to reassure him. She didn't

want him to think she needed help. But she wasn't very successful.

"Uh-huh," was his only comment, but then he leaned over and caressed her lips with his.

Chapter Eight

Was he losing his mind?

Matt ran his fingers through his hair. He'd already tossed his Stetson on the seat beside him. He felt as if he was about to explode.

He was an idiot! He had to be to have kissed Elizabeth. Not that she wasn't kissable. He'd already noted a surprising sexiness in her.

But he hadn't kissed her because she was sexy. He'd kissed her because she'd looked so guilty that she didn't have the nursery all ready for her baby.

Damn it, the woman had dealt with a lot. Much better than he had. Here she was pregnant, her husband dead, she'd made a move, and she thought she should have everything done. She was being too hard on herself.

Julie would've managed.

Before he let that thought take hold, he denied it. He didn't know whether she would've managed. She had been a hard worker, but she had a large support system. Her family hadn't lived too far away, and he and all his family had helped her with whatever she wanted.

Elizabeth had no one.

And she never even complained.

He'd tried to help her. He could give himself credit for that, at least. But now she probably wouldn't let him within a mile of her.

Because he'd kissed her.

Her lips had been soft, pliant, warm.

He shut his memories down. She was seven months pregnant, damn it, with another man's baby. He certainly wasn't desperate enough to hit on a mother-to-be.

He'd wanted to comfort her. That was all. Comfort. And he would continue to do that, but in other ways.

No kissing.

He reached home and strode into the house, his mind on Elizabeth.

"Took you long enough," Willie said, sitting, as usual, at the kitchen table.

He winced. He'd actually planned to stay all night with Elizabeth, once he'd discovered she was at the hospital. But that plan had gone by the wayside after the kiss.

"Uh, yeah." He paced the kitchen, making his way around the big room several times. "Uh, Willie?"

"Yep? What's on your mind, Matt?"

"After...after Julie and the baby were killed, what happened to everything in the nursery?"

Willie froze, as if unsure what she'd heard, but

he waited patiently. Finally, with a sigh, she said, "Your ma and I moved everything to the attic. She said it would be easier on you if you didn't have to look at all of it."

"Is it still there?"

"'Course it is. It's waitin' for the children you'll have in the future."

"I have another idea."

A POUNDING ON HER DOOR brought Elizabeth awake Saturday afternoon. Disoriented by the bright sunlight, she squinted at her watch. Two o'clock.

Since she'd been up and down all night, she'd come home and fallen into bed.

The pounding resumed, along with a loud, deep voice.

"Elizabeth?"

Matt. The way he'd hurried from the hospital last night, as if he thought she would drag him down the aisle on the strength of that one gentle kiss, she hadn't expected him to come around again.

She struggled to her feet, not bothering to put on shoes. At least she was dressed, even if the maternity pants and top were wrinkled. Shoving her hair back from her eyes, she hurried down the hall.

"I'm coming," she called.

He must've heard her because the pounding and yelling stopped.

She didn't bother to look out the peephole, since she knew Matt was her visitor. So when she opened the door, she was surprised to see Willie standing beside him.

"Hello! I'm sorry. I was asleep."

"I thought you'd be up by now," Matt said, frowning.

She held up her hand. "Don't ask me if I'm sick, Matt McIntyre. I'm fine."

"Good. How's Barbie and the baby?"

"They're fine, too, and home now."

"Good," he returned with a satisfied nod. "No more all-nighters, then."

She crossed her arms and glared at him. "Is this a social call, or are you just checking my schedule? I could post it on the porch so you wouldn't have to bother with knocking."

Matt wasn't fazed by her sarcasm. With a grin, he turned to his housekeeper. "See, I told you she didn't appreciate me."

He found no support from Willie.

"Who would, with the racket you've been making? May we come in, Dr. Elizabeth?"

"Of course, Willie. I'm sorry. You must be frozen." She stepped back from the door. "My house isn't very tidy, I'm afraid."

"I've brought the names of three ladies you might want to interview. They're all good women who can help you." Willie pulled a piece of paper out of her coat pocket.

Elizabeth felt tears pool in her eyes. What was wrong with her? But she knew. Everything had gotten to be too much for her. She'd been strong for everyone. Now she was caving in, with her approaching due date. What rotten timing.

"Thank you so much, Willie. I do need help."

"'Course you do. And Matt here has a good idea."

He'd followed them into the living room, closing the door behind him and remaining silent.

She finally looked at him. "What idea?"

For once, Matt didn't look as though he wanted to be in charge. Was it because he was embarrassed by the kiss?

"I—we brought you some things." He looked anywhere but at her.

Willie touched her arm, drawing Elizabeth's attention. Matt's housekeeper smiled at her and nodded, but Elizabeth wasn't sure what she was trying to tell her.

"What things?"

"Baby things," Matt replied. "We…we had some spare baby things and thought you could put them to good use." Without waiting for her to respond, he turned and left the house.

She looked at Willie, now realizing what the woman had been doing. "His— I mean, his and Julie's baby things?"

"Yep. He came home last night and asked where they were. First time he ever said anything. We'd packed everything up in the attic. He never said a word."

"Oh, my," Elizabeth whispered, those tears coming back to her eyes. "Oh, my."

Matt shoved the door open, a big box in his arms.

"Some of these things are for...for boys. But I thought you might know some lady who could use them."

"Of course. It's so generous of you. Set the box down here," she said, clearing off the coffee table.

"There's a crib and chest of drawers and...other things. What room are you using for the baby?"

Her little house only had two bedrooms. "The one across the hall from mine. But I haven't cleaned it. I mean—"

"That's why I came along," Willie assured her. "You start sorting through the box, and I'll have the room cleaned in no time."

"I can't let you do all the work, Willie. That wouldn't be right. I'll come—"

"Sit down," Matt ordered in gruff tones.

"You can't come in my house and tell me what to do!" she snapped, her temper short with all her emotions erupting.

"Go bring in another load, Matthew," Willie ordered.

He glared at Elizabeth, then did as his housekeeper ordered.

"Well!" Elizabeth huffed.

"Now, young lady, you sit down. You can sort through the box if you want, but that's all you're allowed to do."

"But, Willie—"

"Nope. No argument. Or I'll call in reinforcements."

Elizabeth collapsed on the sofa. She was too tired to fight. Willie headed for the second bedroom.

The front door opened again and Matt came through it, pieces of the crib in his arms. He saw her on the sofa and grinned. "You had to obey Willie, too, didn't you? She's a tiger when she wants to be."

Elizabeth couldn't help smiling back. "She threatened to bring in reinforcements. What does that mean?"

"Probably an entire army of women like her. She knows everyone in the county."

"I figured," Elizabeth responded, her mind on the woman in the other room. "I was going to ask her to—" She cut herself off, her hand flying to her mouth. She certainly hadn't intended to inform Matt that she was going to ask Willie to find a woman for him.

"What? What were you going to ask her?"

She tried to think fast. "Uh, to…to find a house-keeper for me."

He stared at her, not quite sure he believed her, she guessed, but then he nodded. "She beat you to it with that list of hers. She usually figures out what I need before I do."

Elizabeth nodded in silent agreement while she opened the box he'd put on the coffee table. She would have to stand to see what was in it, it was so big, but that was preferable to continuing the conversation with Matt.

"I…I really appreciate your offering these things, Matt. I hope it didn't— I mean, I know it must've been hard for—"

"No point in them sitting in my attic gathering

dust when there are babies needing them.'' His voice was gruff, as it had been when he'd ordered her to sit down. But then he added, in softer tones, ''I kind of like the idea of Sarah Beth sleeping in this bed.''

She blinked several times. ''Me, too,'' she said gently, keeping her gaze on the box.

Willie came back into the living room, breaking the silence. ''I need my cleaning supplies, Matt. Did you bring them in yet?''

''No, I'll go get them.''

He left the house again, and Elizabeth drew a deep breath.

Willie patted her on the shoulder. ''You okay? I hope you don't mind secondhand things. It seemed like a good idea for him to do this.''

''Oh, Willie, it's wonderful,'' she assured the older woman. ''And I'm so pleased. I really haven't had time to prepare much. I mean, there's been so much going on.''

''You've had too much resting on your shoulders. We won't do anything you don't like, but we'd like to help you.''

Elizabeth gave the woman a hug. She couldn't help herself. Willie was such a dear.

''Hey, how come Willie gets all the appreciation?'' Matt protested from the door.

His teasing was a relief to Elizabeth. ''I appreciate your help, Matt, more than you'll ever know,'' she assured him as he stopped beside them.

''Then I reckon you'd better give him a hug, too,'' Willie said and stared at the two of them.

Elizabeth stared back, sure she was teasing, but Willie didn't smile. She just waited.

After last night, Elizabeth didn't think Matt would be interested in any close interaction. But he didn't move away. Finally she reached for his shoulders and leaned closer, touching her cheek against his. "Thanks, Matt."

Before she could move away, he pulled her closer, until her stomach rested against his flat, muscular body, his arms wrapped around her.

"My pleasure, Elizabeth. Now sit down and rest." And he was out the door again.

BY SUNSET, Elizabeth had a nursery. A charming crib, with its new mattress, stood near the window. A matching chest of drawers was against one wall. An area rug in bright, primary colors covered the floor.

Inside the chest were baby clothes, nightgowns, T-shirts, socks, bath towels, everything Sarah would need.

Elizabeth would still need to buy some curtains for the window and some little-girl accents, but she had everything else required for a baby.

"It's beautiful," she exclaimed as she and Willie and Matt stood at the door. "Both Sarah and I thank you."

"Pretty name," Willie said, smiling at her.

Matt was scanning the room, as if seeking something. "We're going to call her Sarah Beth."

He turned to find both women staring at him. "What?"

"Don't you think the mother should decide?" Willie asked him.

He frowned. "Decide what? You mean the name? Well, someone suggested—I think it was Bailey—that we call her that and, yeah, of course. It's Elizabeth's decision." His cheeks turned red.

Elizabeth touched his arm. "I think she'll love being called Sarah Beth."

He smiled back, his eyes twinkling, and covered her hand with his. "I hope so."

"I'll go start dinner," Willie said, all business.

Before she could get far, however, Matt stopped her. "Just store all that food we brought, Willie. I'm taking both you ladies out for a steak."

"You brought food?" Elizabeth asked, not having realized some of the things they'd carried in had been food.

"Yep. I was going to cook for all of us, but I don't mind a steak if you don't." Willie waited for her response.

"Of course I don't mind a steak. In fact," Elizabeth added, "*I'll* treat you both to the biggest steaks we can find. I owe you so much."

"It was my invitation," Matt insisted. "So I reckon I'll do the buying. My reputation would suffer if anyone knew I was letting a woman buy me dinner."

"Especially a pregnant woman," Willie added, grinning.

Elizabeth tried to cover her laughter, but when Matt joined in, she chuckled out loud. "I'm not sure it will look any better if *he* buys *me* a dinner, Willie.''

''I think I'll manage to survive,'' Matt assured her. ''Let's get our coats and head out. I'm starving.''

Soon the three of them were in Matt's truck. ''Where are we going?'' Elizabeth asked.

''How about The Way Station? Jeff's got a great chef,'' Matt suggested.

Elizabeth hesitated. ''But more people will see us there.''

''Did you take our teasing seriously?'' Matt asked, frowning.

''No, but—''

''The Way Station it is,'' he growled and wheeled into the hotel parking lot, as if her protest had made the decision for them.

She turned to the other female for support. ''Willie, I didn't mean—''

''Don't worry about it, dearie. They have the best steaks. This is my choice, too.''

Elizabeth accepted the inevitable.

MATT WAVED TO JEFF as they entered the warmly lit lobby.

He hurried over. ''Hello. What are you doing here?''

''We're here to order some big steaks,'' Matt assured him with a grin.

Jeff grinned back. ''Right this way. I'll pick them out special for you. Bailey and I were going to eat upstairs, but we can join you if—''

"Nope. Don't interrupt your privacy. We'll be fine," Matt assured him. He certainly wouldn't be that generous if he was going to have some privacy with—anyone, he hastily added to himself.

"Well, the meal's on the house, then."

"Not on your life. You're running a business here."

"Yeah," Jeff agreed, "but you supply the meat." Without waiting for another argument, he led the way into the restaurant.

Matt was pleased that they had a table waiting, since Saturday night was the most popular dining-out night in Bison City. Not that there were all that many people in Bison City, but then there weren't all that many restaurants, either.

They did a lot of handshaking as they made their way to the table, and attracted a lot of stares. He hadn't been seen much in public with a woman since Julie's death. Even Willie's company wouldn't stop the rumors.

Tough. He wasn't going to let wagging tongues stop him. Besides, being Elizabeth's escort wouldn't hurt his reputation. She was a beautiful woman.

With soft lips.

Damn, he wasn't going to think of that.

After they sat down and picked up the menus, Elizabeth leaned forward. "Everyone's staring."

"I think it's my new hairdo," Willie said casually, patting her hair, which was drawn back in a gray bun the way she always wore it.

Elizabeth let a chuckle escape, and Matt laughed.

"Thank you, Willie," she said softly.

"Or it could be my new boots," Matt added. "They're showstoppers."

"Could be my petticoat is showin'. Some folks don't know it's rude to stare."

Elizabeth couldn't believe the generosity of the two people with her. Their attempts to relieve any tension were quite successful. As Matt opened his mouth to make another outrageous suggestion, she held up her hand. "Stop," she ordered, still laughing. "I can't take any more."

"Good. 'Cause there's nothing more important than a man's boots," he assured her in mock seriousness.

"Right. What kind of steak should I order? I assume you're an expert on steaks," she added, hoping to distract him.

"Yes, ma'am." He went down the menu, telling her the benefits of each cut of meat. Finally she turned helplessly to Willie. "He's giving me too many choices, Willie. What should I order?"

"The Cowgirl. Good cut of meat, small size. It always fills me up," the woman said authoritatively.

"Perfect. Thank you, Willie."

Matt hung his head. "I tried to help."

She almost bought his pose, but then she saw the twinkle in his blue eyes. "Matt McIntyre, you are such a tease."

"Josie would agree with you," Willie added.

"I'm hurt," Matt said, laying his hand on his chest in innocence.

The waiter appeared at the table, rescuing Elizabeth from any more teasing.

Later, after a delicious meal, they were leaving the restaurant when Willie greeted two ladies sitting near the door. Matt and Elizabeth strolled out into the lobby to wait for her.

She came hurrying after them. "Matt, would you run Elizabeth home first? I'd like a few minutes to visit with Violet and Patsy. I haven't seen them in weeks."

Matt could only agree. "Sure. I'll be back in a few minutes."

After shrugging into their coats, Matt took Elizabeth's arm and hurried her out into the cold to his waiting truck.

"I should've come outside and warmed it up for you," he muttered after he slid behind the wheel. "Sorry, Elizabeth. If you want to go back inside, I'll—"

"Matt, it's okay. I've been cold before. You'll have me home before it warms up."

She was right. In two minutes they stopped in front of her house. She turned to thank Matt again for his generosity, but he'd already gotten out of the truck. She opened her door and he was there to help her down.

"You shouldn't have gotten out. I'll be fine."

He ignored her, taking her arm and hurrying her up the sidewalk. When they reached the porch, she dug out her keys.

Her hand was shaking from the cold, and he took the keys from her and opened her door. As they stepped inside, the warm air enveloped them, and she let out a chattering sigh.

"Mmm, that feels good. I'd offer you a cup of tea, but since Willie's—"

"Thanks, I'd like one," he said, stepping around her and heading for the kitchen. "I didn't get to stay and drink the last cup you offered."

"That wasn't my fault," she protested. "Won't Willie worry about you?"

"She won't even notice I'm not back. That woman doesn't stop talking once she gets together with her friends."

"She's a dear. I can't believe all the work she did today."

"She worries about you doing too much," he assured her gravely.

"You can't fool me, Matt McIntyre. *You're* the one who worries. You're worse than a mother hen."

"Yeah," he muttered, not bothering to protest her conclusion. When the kettle whistled, he filled two cups, then followed her lead and added cream and sugar. A surprised look was on his face when he sipped the tea. "That's almost as good as cocoa."

"That's the cream. Though I don't have it too often, since it's so fattening."

"You need to indulge yourself more, Elizabeth."

"I'm not a McIntyre, Matt," she reminded him. "You aren't supposed to boss me around."

"You may not be a McIntyre by name, but we're adopting you. Me and Willie decided."

"The rest of your family may protest," she warned.

"Nah. Besides, I don't have another brother for you to marry, like Bailey and Annie, so I'll just count you as a little sister, like Josie."

Elizabeth wasn't sure why his words depressed her, but she was suddenly tired.

"So from now on," he said, smiling at her, "I'll be checking in on you and Sarah Beth. Get used to it."

Chapter Nine

Elizabeth managed to avoid Matt for several days. She thought that was a good strategy, because she'd figured out why his words Saturday night had depressed her.

For the first time in her life, she was falling in love with a man.

That thought sent panic through her.

She'd loved Dale as her husband and as her friend. He'd understood her absorption with her career, made allowances for her lack of domesticity. They'd planned a future where they both could pursue their careers.

Now that traitorous rush of feeling was centered on an old-fashioned man. A man who's first wife had been a homebody, perfect in every way.

"You idiot!" she chastised herself.

Time to take steps to avoid a life of misery, not measuring up to Matt's standards.

After her Monday morning appointments, she stopped at Nell's for a late lunch. It was after the noon rush, and she hoped to have a talk with Nell.

"Howdy, Dr. Elizabeth," Nell greeted her with a big smile. "You're lookin' better today, more rested."

Elizabeth agreed, sliding into a booth. "Do you have a minute, Nell? I'd like to talk to you about something."

Nell looked around the café, noting the sparseness of customers. "I guess I can visit with you without causin' any problems. Tell me what you want for lunch first."

Elizabeth hurriedly ordered, then waited for Nell's return. Her stomach was queasy, but she didn't know if it was because of Sarah Beth or what she intended to say to Nell.

The older woman came back, sliding into the booth. "Now, what's on your mind, Dr. Elizabeth? Need a donation for the hospital?"

"Oh, no, Nell. I think the Millennium Baby Contest is going to raise a lot of money." She paused, pressing her lips together. Finally she said, "My request is…is personal."

Nell raised one eyebrow but said nothing.

"It's Matt."

"Matt McIntyre?" Nell asked, as if there was more than one Matt in Bison City.

"Yes," Elizabeth nodded. "I wondered if you knew any ladies who might—you know, be interested in Matt."

Nell leaned back in the booth and roared with laughter. When she finally stopped chuckling, she leaned forward. "Are you joking?"

Elizabeth shook her head. "No, I'm not. Really,'' she added as Nell chuckled again. ''He needs encouragement and I thought—''

''Lord have mercy, child, the problem isn't finding a woman interested in Matt. It's Matt being interested in a woman.''

One of the waitresses brought over two plates of the luncheon special, chicken and dumplings today, and set them in front of Elizabeth and Nell. With a smile, she then hurried into the kitchen.

''She's your new waitress, isn't she? I thought maybe—she's very pretty. Matt might like her.''

''She's got a boyfriend. And besides, she's not ready to settle down.''

''Oh. Well, whoever she is, she'll need to know about ranching, how to bake, how to quilt, and…and whatever else Julie was good at.'' She took a drink of tea. ''Do you know someone like that?''

''Not anyone alive,'' Nell said with a dryness that startled Elizabeth.

She stared at the woman, her mouth open.

Nell nodded. ''I didn't mean anything bad, but Julie wasn't perfect, Doctor. Matt's memory may have turned her into the perfect wife, but she wasn't. But she loved her man, and tried to do everything she could for him. She spoiled him rotten.''

''I gathered that,'' Elizabeth agreed with a faint smile. ''And I think that's what he's looking for in his next wife.''

''Probably. But that don't mean he'd be happy.''

Elizabeth decided to ignore Nell's opinion. "But do you know anyone like that?"

"Maybe."

"Will you throw them together?"

Nell studied her, making her uncomfortable, but finally she said, "I'll see what I can do, but I'm no Cupid."

MATT HUNG UP THE PHONE, a puzzled frown on his face.

"Who was it?" Willie asked.

He turned to stare suspiciously at his house-keeper. "It was Nell. She issued a personal invitation to dine at the Chuck Wagon Café this evening. Said she'd already talked to you."

"Yep. She's trying out a new recipe tonight. Wants us to give her our opinion. You don't mind, do you?"

With a sigh Matt nodded. "I guess not. But I don't plan to linger. I'm tired tonight." He gave Willie another sharp look, then added, "I'll go clean up. Be ready to leave in twenty minutes."

She nodded, smiling.

Matt had almost reached the stairs when he whirled around. "I'll call Elizabeth. She should join us."

Willie's eyes widened in surprise, but she didn't say anything. Matt shrugged. Willie liked Elizabeth. There would be no objection from her.

When Elizabeth answered the phone, he got a rush of pleasure, satisfaction, that surprised him. "How you doing?"

"Matt? I'm doing fine."

"Good. Willie and I are eating at Nell's tonight. Why don't you join us?"

"You are? Is Willie sick?"

"Nope. Nell wants us to try out a new recipe. We'll pick you up in half an hour."

"Wait!" she called as he started to hang up the phone. "I'm not dressed. I don't think—"

"You can get dressed. Nell needs us. See you in half an hour." He hung up the phone before she could protest again, a smile on his lips.

When he and Willie reached Elizabeth's little house, she was ready. He escorted her to the truck where Willie was waiting.

"What recipe is Nell cooking tonight?" Elizabeth asked.

"She didn't say," Matt responded. "Do you know, Willie?"

"It's a southwest chicken casserole. She picked it up on her trip to Texas. Kinda a mix of Mexican and Southern."

"That sounds delicious," Elizabeth said.

Matt watched her out of the corner of his eye as she rubbed her stomach. "Mexican won't upset Sarah Beth?"

"I don't think so."

"There'll probably be a crowd tonight," Willie said, "so we might have to share a booth with someone else."

Matt looked at his housekeeper, finding her words strange, but she stared straight ahead.

"Okay. We're friendly folks," he finally said.

It seemed Willie was right. The café was almost completely filled. But Nell had saved the big booth in the back, that held six, for them.

"Welcome, folks. Glad you could make it," she greeted them with a smile. "Come on back. I saved this spot for you three, but I may have to seat some others with you. Business is booming."

Matt raised one eyebrow. During the week, there weren't that many diners in Bison City. Then he caught sight of the sign plastered on the wall, and he understood. Half-price Night.

When they reached the booth, Willie slid in first. As Elizabeth was about to follow, Matt took her arm and guided her to the other side.

"I was going to sit with Willie," she protested.

"It'll be more balanced if you sit on this side," he assured her, hoping she didn't challenge his logic. He didn't want to have to explain that he liked having her near him.

Since they didn't need to read the menus, the three of them were chatting about the Millennium Baby Contest, when Nell returned to their table, accompanied by two women.

"Willie, look who's here," she announced. "Your old friend Alma Carter and her niece Cathy. You don't mind if they join you, do you?"

"A'course not," Willie replied, gesturing for them to sit down.

Matt nodded to the two women as they slid in beside Willie, noting that the younger woman was a looker. The way her gaze roved over him had him drawing back, though. You'd think he was prime rib and the woman was starving.

Willie introduced everyone, indicating that Elizabeth was the doctor who would deliver all the babies.

"Looks like you've got one on the way yourself," Cathy said with a smile. "Who's going to deliver yours?"

"Dr. Gardner, my partner," Elizabeth returned.

Cathy nodded, then turned to Matt. "Are you the father of the baby?"

Elizabeth's cheeks turned red and Matt gave the other woman a hard stare. "No. Elizabeth is a widow."

He was concerned about Elizabeth's embarrassment, but he didn't mind the thought of being Sarah Beth's father. Any man would be proud to be her daddy.

"Oh, I'm sorry," Cathy cooed. "I just naturally thought since you were together— I mean, are you dating?"

"No," Elizabeth said and picked up her glass of water to take a sip. "Matt's a friend…and a bachelor."

Cathy smiled at him. "Aunt Alma said there were a lot of available men around here."

Matt didn't like the way the conversation was going. He slanted a smile at Elizabeth. "There may be one less soon."

"Are you thinking of settling in Bison City?" Willie hurriedly asked.

"I'd like to. I'm looking for a teaching job. I'm a home economics teacher."

Matt chuckled. "Maybe you can teach Elizabeth to cook," he teased. Immediately he realized his mistake when Elizabeth colored up again. "Sorry, honey, I was just teasing," he hurriedly added.

"You can't cook?" Cathy asked in disbelief. "Every woman should know how to cook. It keeps a man happy," she added, smiling at Matt. "Why, I win prizes for my cooking all the time."

"Congratulations," Elizabeth murmured. "Do you sew, too? Make quilts, things like that?"

"Oh, yes. Sewing is such a pleasure, taking a piece of material and creating something out of nothing. It's becoming a lost art." Cathy looked at Elizabeth. "Do you sew?"

"Only on my patients," Elizabeth said coolly.

Matt's laughter was interrupted by Nell's arrival with their dinners. It seemed everyone at the table was having the new special.

Conversation dwindled as they ate. Matt had put in a full day's work and had worked up a big appetite. Usually Willie had food waiting for him when he came in. That's why tonight was so unusual.

He remembered being suspicious earlier when Nell had called. And even before that when he'd come into the kitchen, surprised to find no dinner. Before he'd been able to ask Willie about it, the phone had rung.

He supposed she and Nell had worked everything out earlier, so they could try the new recipe. And it was good. Nell came by the table to get their opinions.

Everyone but Cathy praised the meal. She, however, had a different opinion. "It's very good, Nell, but I think just a tince more cayenne pepper would spice it up. And maybe more onions, too. It would give it a more distinctive flavor. Right now it's a little too...bland." She beamed at the woman, as if waiting for approval of her rating.

Nell glowered. "Don't want it too spicy. Unsettles some folks' stomachs."

"Well, of course, it's your restaurant," Cathy returned, stating the obvious.

Nell moved on and Alma leaned forward. "Isn't Cathy talented? She's going to make some man a wonderful wife. Why, there isn't anything she can't do. She was even raised on a farm, knows about animals and all."

"She's incredibly talented," Elizabeth agreed. "She'll make a perfect rancher's wife."

Matt blinked as all four women seemed to be staring at him. Realization set in. He'd been set up. Well, they could think again. He wasn't ready for another wife.

He put down his fork and laid his arm along the back of the booth, around Elizabeth. "We'll have to look around for an interested rancher, won't we, honey?" he suggested, smiling at Elizabeth. "We wouldn't want all that talent to get away from Bison City."

Elizabeth stared at him, her eyes blank with astonishment.

Cathy began, "But I thought—"

Alma stared at him.

Willie continued eating. "Best ask Nell. She knows most everyone in Bison City."

Since he figured it was Willie and Nell who had hatched the matchmaking plan, he waved for Nell's attention. She hurried over to the table.

"You need seconds, Matt?"

"Nope, Nell, though I really liked this dish. I wouldn't turn down a piece of cherry pie."

She asked if anyone else was interested in dessert. After the others declined, she started to hurry away, but Matt stopped her.

"By the way, Cathy here is thinking she might like to stay in Bison City. You know any ranchers needing a wife?"

It wasn't often Nell was struck silent. She moved her mouth several times, but nothing came out.

Elizabeth hurried to her rescue. "I'm sure someone as lovely and talented as Cathy won't have any trouble meeting men in Bison City. They're all so friendly," she added, smiling at the embarrassed young woman.

"Yeah," Matt agreed robustly. "I met Elizabeth just a couple of weeks ago. It's amazing how fast things can happen."

Both Willie and Elizabeth stared at him again, but the two newcomers kept their gazes fastened on their plates.

"Uh, I'll get that pie for you," Nell said before she walked away.

"I hope I didn't embarrass you, Cathy," Matt

said calmly. "But Nell likes to help people. Sometimes even when she shouldn't." He sent Willie a hard look.

Elizabeth cleared her throat. "I'm sure Nell meant well."

"Aw, honey, you always give everyone the benefit of the doubt," he said and pulled her against him, dropping a kiss on her startled lips.

She glared at him and scooted closer to the window.

Nell returned with the pie, and he took his arm down from behind Elizabeth. But he missed her warmth. "Want a bite?"

"No, thank you. I'm watching my weight."

"I hear you have to be careful not to gain a lot of weight when you're pregnant," Cathy commented. "I don't look forward to losing my figure, but I love little babies."

Matt thought Elizabeth didn't have much to worry about. She had a natural slenderness that even her pregnancy couldn't hide.

"I guess losing my tiny waist for a few months will be worth it," Cathy added, putting her hand to that part of her body.

Matt frowned. The woman was growing obvious, and probably making Elizabeth feel bad. He said, "Elizabeth doesn't have to worry. If anything, she probably needs to gain a few pounds."

"Playing doctor again, are we?" Elizabeth muttered under her breath.

Matt leaned toward her and whispered, "Anytime with you, Elizabeth.'' Then he chuckled when her cheeks flamed.

''Matt, behave yourself,'' Willie ordered.

''Yes, ma'am,'' he agreed with an innocent look before he turned his attention to his pie.

THINGS WEREN'T GOING as well as Elizabeth had hoped.

Nell had called her earlier in the day, telling her she'd found the perfect woman for Matt.

Elizabeth had been depressed the rest of the day.

When Matt had invited her to join them at the café, she'd known she should refuse. After all, the contrast between the perfect woman for Matt and her would be even more depressing. But she hadn't been able to resist.

Matt, however, hadn't fallen all over the perfect woman. In fact, as the evening progressed, he seemed to grow less and less interested in Cathy.

And he was using Elizabeth as a weapon.

Suddenly her stomach reacted to all the turmoil.

''Um, I'm sorry. I— Excuse me!'' she said desperately, shoving against Matt, hoping he'd get the message quickly.

He slid out of the booth, taking her arm to help her out. She was grateful. Then she hurried to the rest room.

When Willie entered only a couple of minutes later, she was feeling a little better, but she'd lost most of her dinner.

''You okay, Dr. Elizabeth?''

"Yes, just a queasy stomach. Sorry, Willie. I shouldn't have come."

Willie shrugged. "Matt didn't give you much choice. Anyway, it's been interesting."

Elizabeth sighed. "But it's not working, is it? Maybe it's still too soon. But I thought—"

"It wasn't a bad idea," Willie said, patting her on her shoulder consolingly. "The boy's unpredictable."

"But I don't understand. She's everything Julie was. Why isn't he interested?"

"I reckon it's that chemistry thing all the ladies' magazines talk about. Some folks just don't hit you right." Willie looked at her. "Frankly, if he married miss perfect, I'd have to quit, anyway, so I'm glad it didn't take."

"Why?"

"That woman would be the queen bee of the kitchen. There wouldn't be any room for me."

Elizabeth hugged Willie. "Then I'm glad he didn't like her, because Matt can't do without you."

When they came out of the rest room, arm in arm, they found Matt leaning against the wall, waiting for them.

"Why aren't you at the table?" Willie demanded.

Matt cocked one eyebrow. "I was worried about Elizabeth. Besides, I didn't want to exchange recipes with Cathy Carter. The woman can't seem to talk about anything but her accomplishments."

Elizabeth and Willie exchanged a look.

When Matt's arm went around Elizabeth's shoulders, her gaze was drawn back to him.

"You okay?"

"I'm fine," she hurriedly said, moving away from his hold. It felt too good, too comfortable. She mustn't get used to his touch.

"Come on, we'll take you home. Do you still have milk?"

She looked at him in exasperation. "Matt, you don't have to—"

"I told you we adopted you. Wouldn't milk be good for her, Willie?"

"Probably some soda would be better, to settle her stomach," Willie suggested. "We can stop by the store on the way home and pick some up."

Elizabeth rolled her eyes but gave up. "I have soda at home. Just drop me off and I'll be fine."

Matt had already paid the bill, including Alma and Cathy Carter's, and he escorted Willie and Elizabeth to his truck after telling Nell goodbye.

Elizabeth gave Nell a wry smile, trying to convey her appreciation for Nell's efforts even if they didn't work. She'd stop by tomorrow to make sure Nell understood.

Nell wasn't the only one Elizabeth had enlisted in her campaign to find a woman for Matt. Josie, Annie and Bailey had all promised to be on the lookout. Maybe their efforts would be more successful.

Matt insisted on escorting her to her door.

"You sure you don't want us to come in for a while, to be sure you're okay?"

"I'll be fine, Matt, I promise."

"Okay. I'm not sure what was going on tonight at the café. I think Nell may have been matchmaking. It's weird."

"Uh, yeah."

"Well, good night, Elizabeth."

To her surprise he pulled her against him for a hug. Unprepared, she had no time to put her hands between them as a barrier. Instead she was engulfed in his warm muscles. Sarah Beth must've liked the idea, because she beat a tattoo on Matt's stomach.

Again Matt kissed her on her lips, as if it were a habit. It sent her pulses racing.

"Call if you need anything." After releasing her, he patted her stomach. "Be good, Sarah Beth." Then he headed back to his truck.

"Oh, my, Sarah Beth, we are in deep trouble," she murmured to her child. "Neither one of us is any good at resisting Matt McIntyre."

She'd better work on that resistance. If she didn't, she and Sarah Beth might have to move away from Bison City. And she really didn't want to go.

Chapter Ten

Elizabeth didn't get any help from Bailey in finding a woman to interest Matt. She got word she'd won a designing contest in New York. Then she had a television interview on a Denver station about the Millennium Baby Contest that increased the amount of entries and donations.

As Bailey prepared for her trip to New York to accept her award, Josie tried to deal with all the incoming mail. Elizabeth and Annie went over one evening to help her out.

"Wow!" Elizabeth finally said after staring at the two mail bags in the corner of Josie's dining room.

"I can't believe it," Annie added. "There's money in all those envelopes?"

"I sure hope so," Josie returned. "Thanks for coming to help. Let me show you the system Bailey and I set up."

In a short period of time they had an assembly line going. Elizabeth, wielding a wicked letter opener, slit open each envelope, noted the amount enclosed on the entry form or letter and passed it on to Annie. She recorded the name and address and what they entered. Josie recorded the money or check in a ledger, along with the person's name, and filled out a confirmation form to be mailed back.

When Justin arrived a few minutes later, he began stuffing envelopes and addressing them.

"We'll get through all of it, the way we're moving," Josie said excitedly. "When Bailey gets back from New York, she won't believe how much we've gotten done."

"Are you sure she's coming back?" Justin asked quietly.

All three ladies stared at him. Finally Elizabeth asked faintly, "You don't mean that, do you?"

He shrugged his shoulders. Annie and Elizabeth turned to Josie.

"Don't look at me. I don't know what he's talking about. Justin, spill it."

"I don't know anything for sure. But I had a conversation with Matt and he, well, he was concerned that once Bailey got to New York, she wouldn't want to come back."

"Oh, that's just Matt. He's always looking on the dark side," Josie said, leaning back in relief.

"Jeff told him it was possible."

All three ladies gasped, then Josie moaned, "Poor Jeff."

"Yeah, 'cause he hates New York City," Justin agreed.

"Wait a minute," Elizabeth said. "You don't mean Jeff would move to New York, too?"

Justin nodded his head, adding, "He loves her."

After a moment of stunned silence, all three women broke into protest, but Justin held up his hand. "I don't know anything for sure. Just what Matt said."

"Well, I refuse to believe Bailey would do that," Josie finally said, her voice shaky.

"Me, too," Annie agreed.

Elizabeth said nothing. She·hoped the other two were right, but who could tell? Stranger things had happened.

"On the lighter side, Matt told me something else," Justin said, again drawing their attention.

"I hope this is better news," Josie complained.

"Well, it's amusing, at least." Justin clasped his hands together on the table, giving up all pretense to working. "Nell tried to matchmake Matt with a new lady in town."

"No!" Annie protested in surprise.

"Really?" Josie asked, but her gaze strayed to Elizabeth's face. "Did she do okay?"

"Nope. Matt didn't like the lady."

Elizabeth kept silent, not raising her gaze from her work.

"Elizabeth?" Josie said. "Do you know anything about this matchmaking?"

With a sigh Elizabeth looked at her friend and patient. "Yes. I guess I'm going to have to confess to Matt to get Nell off the hook. She tried the matchmaking because I asked her to."

"How did you know, Josie?" Justin asked.

"Because Elizabeth asked me to find someone for Matt, too," Josie said.

"Me, too," Annie added, staring at Elizabeth.

Justin smiled. "You're mighty anxious to see Matt married again."

"I thought you wanted him to be happy," Elizabeth exclaimed.

"Of course we do!" Josie exclaimed in return.

"Well, Cathy Carter won't make him happy," Justin assured her. "I've met the woman."

"What's wrong with her?" Elizabeth demanded. "She cooks and sews just like Julie did."

Annie and Josie looked at each other and then at Elizabeth. Josie asked, "Is that what you're looking for, a Julie clone?"

Elizabeth reined in her frustration and said quietly, "No. I'm looking for someone who will make Matt happy. But creature comforts are very important to a man. Right, Justin?"

He held up both hands. "Hey, I don't want to get in the middle of an argument."

"There's no argument," Josie assured him. Then she turned to Elizabeth. "You're right about men loving their creature comforts, but that's not why Matt loved Julie."

"No, of course not. I didn't mean Julie wasn't a wonderful person. But Nell thought— Anyway, Cathy cooks and sews superlatively. She told us."

"Ad nauseam according to Matt," Justin inserted.

"She wasn't that bad," Elizabeth protested.

"And at least Nell tried, which is more than any of the rest of you have done."

Elizabeth was embarrassed by her accusation. She hadn't meant to offend her friends, but when she tried to apologize, Annie stopped her.

"Actually, we talked about it, Josie and I."

"You did? Have you found someone? Or do you not think it's time? Maybe we should wait a week or two, but—"

"Elizabeth," Josie said softly, watching her, "we picked you."

Elizabeth forgot to breathe until she began seeing stars in front of her eyes. Then she took huge gulps of air as she clutched the table. "No," she protested when her breathing was under control. "No, no, no."

"Why not?" Annie asked.

Elizabeth shoved her chair back and stood, gesturing to her rounded stomach. "Look at me! I'm seven months pregnant. Not exactly date bait!"

"Well, I'm not either, but I'm planning on landing me a guy," Annie returned, a smile on her face.

Elizabeth saw the fear in her eyes, too, and her heart went out to Annie. She subsided into her chair. "That's different, Annie. Alex loves you. He's loved you for a long time. And, even if you haven't said it, I believe you're carrying Alex's child."

Annie didn't admit what Elizabeth said was true. She hadn't expected her to. But she reached out a hand to Elizabeth, and they clung to each other.

"Hey, don't leave me out of this," Josie said, putting her hand on top of the others'.

"You won't be pregnant forever," Justin said, looking at Elizabeth.

She drew another deep breath. "No, but I'll still be me."

The other three stared at her.

"And what's wrong with you?" Annie finally asked.

Elizabeth smiled wearily. "Nothing, if you're looking for a doctor. Nothing, if you're looking for a mother, I hope. But if you're looking for a wife, a homemaker, someone who centers her world around her husband, then there's a lot wrong about me."

"I don't see anything wrong," Josie said stubbornly, reminding Elizabeth greatly of her brother.

"Josie, I can't cook!" Elizabeth exclaimed in exasperation. "You should've seen the cherry pie I tried to make for Thanksgiving. It was a disaster. My house is never clean. I forget to do the grocery shopping. I get the cleaners to sew on buttons. Do you think that's what Matt wants in a wife, even if I wasn't pregnant with another man's baby?"

"You did a great job of delivering Barbie's baby," Josie finally said.

"Thank you," Elizabeth agreed with a smile. "I'm a good doctor. I said that. But it would take an extremely liberated man to accept me as a wife." She smiled at her audience. "The men in Bison City are good men. Matt is one of the best. But liberated? Willing to do the dishes after working outside all day? I don't think so.''

''Justin and I share the household chores,'' Josie said, and Justin nodded in confirmation. He reached out and took his wife's hand, sending her a caressing look.

Elizabeth looked away. That closeness, that sharing, caused such yearning in her heart. But she mustn't think about it.

''When Alex was here, he cooked. And helped with all kinds of things,'' Annie said softly.

Even Josie stared in disbelief. ''Alex? Are you sure?''

''Of course I'm sure. He hasn't lived at home much in the last few years. If he waited for Willie to cook his meals, he'd be skin and bones.''

''I hadn't thought about that,'' Josie said, wearing a puzzled look. ''I guess he has had to learn to take care of himself. Well, good for him.''

''Yes, that is good,'' Elizabeth agreed. ''Because after you have the baby, you'll need someone to help out for a while.''

''If he comes back,'' Annie added.

''He will,'' Josie said firmly. ''Or I'll hunt him down like a dog.''

They all laughed at her words, but it was nervous laughter, as if they all feared she might have to do just that.

''So, see,'' Josie said, ''we've proved you wrong.''

''No, you've proved me wrong about Alex and Justin. Not about Matt.''

"But Matt doesn't do anything around the house because Willie won't let him," Josie argued. "I'm sure he would if he needed to."

Elizabeth decided the argument had gone on long enough. "Look, we need to find the right woman for Matt. If he's not interested in someone because she can cook and sew, then what kind of woman would he be interested in?"

"You!" Josie exclaimed. "He's interested in you! He's spent more time with you than any woman since Julie."

"You're right. He has." Before Josie could exclaim in triumph, Elizabeth added, "That's because he's adopted me as a second little sister. And no matter how much you argue, you can't convince me that a man who thinks of a woman as his little sister has any interest in marrying her."

No one had an argument for that point.

MATT HADN'T BEEN INTO TOWN in several days, not since the fiasco at Nell's café. But the weekend was here. He wanted Elizabeth and Annie to come for Sunday dinner tomorrow.

"Did you invite Elizabeth and Annie for tomorrow?" he asked Willie at dinner that evening.

"I figured you did," Willie said, staring at him.

"I forgot to call them. I'd better do it now."

"You can at least wait until you finish your dinner. I'm not reheating it for you."

Matt sat back down in his chair, though he knew Willie was bluffing. She spoiled him rotten. It wouldn't be the first time she'd warmed up food for him when it was his fault it was cold.

After he'd cleaned his plate and carried it to the sink, he went to the wall phone. First he dialed Annie's number. After several questions about her health, he asked her to return to the ranch after church to have lunch with the family.

She happily accepted.

Everything was nice and simple with Annie.

Then he called Elizabeth.

"Oh, thank you, Matt, but I think I'll stay home."

"Willie will be disappointed. She's making pot roast."

"It sounds delicious, but my appetite isn't what it was. I probably wouldn't do it justice, anyway."

"You're not feeling well?" he demanded instantly, alarm rising in him.

"Matt, I'm fine. Sometimes women don't eat as much in the third trimester. It's perfectly normal."

"Well, what you do eat should be good solid food. You're coming here for lunch tomorrow." And he wasn't going to take no for an answer.

"Matt McIntyre, there you go again! You have no business making decisions for me."

"It's not you I'm bossing around. It's Sarah Beth. She needs a lot of protein. I bet you haven't cooked anything today, have you?"

"No, but I ate at Nell's for lunch and had leftovers for dinner. So there!"

"You mean you prefer Nell's cooking over Willie's,'' Matt said suggestively, staring at Willie. ''I'm afraid you've hurt Willie's feelings.''

''Matt, can Willie hear you?''

''She sure can,'' he said pleasantly.

''I'm going to wring your neck! How dare you say such a thing in front of her.''

''Guess you'll have to come to dinner tomorrow to prove me wrong or Willie won't believe you.''

Silence followed, as if she was weighing her options. Finally, with a sigh, she said, ''Okay, I'm coming tomorrow, but I'm explaining to Willie how you shamelessly tricked me, so don't think you can get away with it again.''

''Yes, ma'am. I'll see you at church.''

He hung up the phone, a smile on his face.

''You're looking mighty pleased with yourself,'' Willie commented.

''Both ladies are coming,'' he offered as a reason.

''I heard. The second one took a little persuading. And what was that about Nell's food?''

Matt took a quick look at his housekeeper and decided to mend fences at once. ''I was teasing Elizabeth. She ate at Nell's today.''

''Hmmm, I wonder if Nell's trying her matchmaking on Elizabeth. There's always a lot of bachelors hanging around there.''

Matt stared at her as if she was a ghost. ''What are you talking about? Why would Nell— Elizabeth isn't— She's pregnant!''

''All the more reason to find her a man.'' Willie

didn't look up as she rinsed the dishes before load-ing them into the dishwasher.

Matt moved to Willie's side. "Has Elizabeth said— I mean, has she mentioned being interested in marrying again? Her husband has only been dead half a year."

"That don't seem like a long time for some, but Elizabeth has had a heavy load to carry all by her-self. I don't think anyone would think less of her if she married now."

"But...but she hasn't met anyone. Has she? Has she mentioned anyone?" His brain was scrambling with the thought of Elizabeth looking for a man, wanting to...to date? Without waiting for Willie to answer his question, he added, "She can't marry a man now. What if Sarah Beth didn't like him?"

"By the time that baby is old enough to vote on the identity of her daddy, Elizabeth might be too old."

"Don't be ridiculous. She's five years younger than me. She'd be in the prime of life," he assured Willie. "She should wait."

"And take care of everything by herself? The baby, her job, the house. It's too much."

Matt stared at Willie. "Why are you saying these things? Do you want her to marry?"

"It's not a question of what I want. But I know about bein' alone. It's not easy."

Matt suddenly realized how much he'd taken his housekeeper for granted. Willie was always there, meeting his every need when it came to home and comfort.

"Willie, are you unhappy?"

She looked at him in surprise. "Who, me? Naw, not since I come here. The McIntyres are my family now. I'm not alone no more. But Elizabeth is."

WILLIE'S WORDS STAYED with Matt. He scarcely heard the sermon the next morning. He was too busy worrying about Elizabeth and her love life.

He'd intended to find her before the service and bring her to sit with him and Willie, Justin and Josie, and, this morning, Annie and Dex. The McIntyre pew.

But the service had already begun when she slipped into the back row. He caught her eye and nodded to her, a smile on his face, until Red Stephens sat down next to her.

Was he one of the men at the café yesterday? The man nodded at Elizabeth, and she smiled in return. Matt ground his teeth, irritation filling him. Had she planned to sit with the man?

Well, he'd have a talk with her this afternoon. Red didn't have that good a reputation with the women. His wife left him a couple of years back. And there was that waitress at Nell's café who'd moved on.

No, Red wasn't the man for Elizabeth.

"Matt, pass the offering plate!" Willie whispered, nudging him in the ribs.

With a start he grabbed the plate and almost overturned it. Nothing fell out, but the coins jangled and several people chuckled. His cheeks red, he stared straight ahead.

He couldn't wait until the service ended.

ELIZABETH MANAGED to ride to the ranch with Josie and Justin. She wasn't sure why Matt was so determined to put her in his truck, but she avoided him until she'd already asked Justin and crawled into the back seat.

"What are you doing in there?" he'd demanded.

"Riding with Justin and Josie," she'd calmly replied.

"Come ride with me and Willie."

"No, it's too much trouble to change now. I'll see you at the ranch." She'd smiled and stayed stubbornly in the back seat.

"Start the car, Justin," Josie said under her breath, "before Matt rips the door off."

Justin waved to Matt and followed Josie's order. "He wouldn't do that," he assured his wife, even as he was watching Matt carefully in his rearview mirror.

"You think not? Steam was coming out his ears." Then she looked over the seat. "Why was he so upset? Have you two had a fight?"

Elizabeth didn't have to pretend innocence. "No. He teased me last night, but he always does that. I haven't even told him that I'm the reason Nell tried to matchmake. I'm dreading that."

"You could keep quiet. Nell won't say anything," Josie said.

"No, that wouldn't be fair."

"Maybe you'd better tell him while the rest of us are around, then," Josie suggested with a sigh.

"Maybe I will."

When they reached the ranch, Matt was waiting for them. He opened the back door and offered a hand to help Elizabeth out while Justin did the same for Josie.

"Lordy, I will be so glad to have this baby and be able to move like regular folks again," Josie said. "No one told me it was going to be so long."

"Now, sweetheart, you know it's the same amount of time for everyone," Justin assured her.

Elizabeth grinned. She didn't think Josie was in the mood to hear those words.

Josie confirmed her suspicions. "Justin Moore, don't try to make it sound like being pregnant is nothing! If men had to carry the baby around the way women do, we'd never have children!"

"Without a doubt," Matt assured his sister, patting her on the shoulder as he retained his hold on Elizabeth's arm. "Justin's a man of logic. He didn't mean any harm."

Justin, a bewildered look on his face, shook his head vigorously. "Of course not, Josie."

"Well, just as long as you understand." She led him away to the house. Justin looked over his shoulder at the other two, as if asking them to please explain what had just happened.

"Poor guy," Matt said with a soft chuckle. "He'll learn how irrational women get when they're pregnant."

"Irrational?" Elizabeth asked, coming to an abrupt halt.

Chapter Eleven

Matt watched Elizabeth as they ate dinner. She was sitting next to Willie at the other end of the table. Was she still upset with his casual remark? He'd hurriedly backed away from his words about irrationality, but only because he didn't want to upset her. After all, he could remember when Julie had tried to pretend that she hadn't gained any weight. He and Willie hadn't challenged her perception of the truth.

"Why are you smiling?" Josie asked.

"What? Oh, I was remembering something Julie used to do," he told her.

"You were? And it made you smile?" Josie asked, as if wanting to confirm what she'd heard.

He frowned impatiently. "Yeah. How's the baby contest coming?"

"I can't believe the amount of money we're going to make. We worked a couple of hours on Friday and collected over three thousand dollars. And we have almost another month."

"I'm impressed, Josie. Good going."

Justin leaned forward. "The girls really have done a good job, all of them."

"You didn't sound so happy about it when you didn't have any clean underwear this morning," Josie reminded him.

Annie covered her smile with her hand. Elizabeth didn't bother, grinning at his sister.

"You think that's funny?" Matt asked her.

"About as funny as irrational behavior," she returned coolly.

Okay, so she hadn't forgiven him. But she was right. There was something amusing about Justin not having clean underwear because his wife was running a baby contest.

"Need some help, Josie?" Willie asked. "I can spare an hour or two to do some laundry."

"It's all right, Willie," Josie replied. "Justin put in a load this morning."

Matt cocked an eyebrow at his brother-in-law. "Well, that's one way to solve the problem."

"Josie didn't feel too well this morning," Justin said, looking at his wife in concern.

Elizabeth leaned forward to look at Josie. "Anything I should know?"

"No," Josie said firmly. "I was tired, that's all. Between the paper and the contest, I guess I overdid it yesterday."

Matt started to warn his sister not to overdo, but Elizabeth was ahead of him. "I think it might be a good idea to organize committees to handle the contest. We're all going to be a little busy around

New Year's. And the contest is going to benefit all the citizens.''

"Good idea," Justin said, enthusiasm in his voice. "I was beginning to wonder how we'd make it to the first of the year. I'll write something up for the paper tomorrow."

"I'll call my friends," Willie added. "At lot of them have time on their hands, since their families are raised. They'd like to be involved."

"We'll need a meeting place," Elizabeth said.

"The newspaper offices are available. We've got the so-called conference room. It has a big table," Justin volunteered.

Matt sat there as everyone around the table got involved, coming up with solutions to difficulties. Elizabeth, once she'd gotten the ball rolling, said little. But he knew it was her finding a solution that had made a difference.

Julie had done a lot, but she hadn't wanted to let anyone else contribute. He'd offered to help her when she'd been baking cookies late at night, but she wouldn't even let him take the cookies off the cookie sheets. She had to do it all herself.

He remembered the friction Julie's attitude had sometimes caused between her and Willie. His housekeeper was easygoing, but she was somewhat proprietorial about her kitchen.

The planning had slowed as everyone seemed to be satisfied. Matt decided it was a good time to do a little work of his own.

"Say, Elizabeth, I didn't know you knew Red Stephens."

Her head snapped up and she stared at him, a frown on her delicate features.

"Red Stephens? I don't think—"

"He sat beside you in church this morning."

The frown was replaced with a puzzled look. "Was that who he was? I don't think I've been introduced to him."

"Oh," Matt said, trying to hide his relief. "I thought maybe you'd met him at Nell's. He's a bachelor, hangs out there a lot."

"No."

"Ah, I see. Willie had wondered if maybe Nell was on a matchmaking kick. Since she tried it with me," he added in explanation. "Thought maybe she was trying the same thing with you."

He was curious when first shock and then guilt filled her face. She'd never make a poker player, he thought with pleasure. Her emotions were always there for everyone to see.

Then he remembered her calm demeanor when delivering Barbie Ward's baby. Maybe he needed to rethink his ideas about Elizabeth.

"Uh, Matt," she called, getting his attention. "I need to tell you something."

His eyes narrowed and his heartbeat sped up. What was it? Had she met someone? Was something wrong with Sarah Beth? "It's my fault Nell tried—introduced you to Cathy Carter."

In the sudden silence Willie added, "And mine."

"No, Willie, there's no need to take part of the blame," Elizabeth protested, a warm smile on her face for his housekeeper.

"I don't understand," Matt said, staring at both women. "Why would either of you encourage Nell to sic a woman like Cathy Carter on me?"

"I suggested to Nell that you might be ready to…to move on. And that you'd be looking for someone who could do all the things Julie was so good at."

Matt stared at her, dumbfounded.

"You know, like cooking and sewing," she added. "Home things."

Matt sat frozen, staring at Elizabeth. Finally, in the silence around them, he said, a harsh burr in his voice, "May I speak with you in my office, Elizabeth?" He shoved his chair back and stood.

"Now, Matt," Willie began.

"Matt, don't be mad at—" Josie protested.

"Elizabeth?" he repeated, since she hadn't moved, cutting off the other two women.

She didn't want to go with him. He could see that in her face. But she was no coward. Standing, she said, her voice controlled, "Of course."

Then she walked out of the room, leaving him staring after her.

Josie stuck her elbow in her husband's side. Matt supposed his sister wanted her husband to offer advice since neither of his brothers was present.

"She meant well," Justin said.

"Yeah," Matt growled and stalked out of the room.

ELIZABETH WAS GLAD Matt didn't immediately follow her. It gave her time to catch her breath.

When he entered the room, she turned to face him, a calmness descending over her. "I'd offer you an apology, except that I think I did the right thing. It just didn't work out."

"And never will with a woman like Cathy Carter," he said.

"But she does all the things Julie did. I thought you would want a woman like that."

"What makes you think I want a woman at all?"

She swallowed her nerves. "Because you're human. Because being alone is difficult. Because life should be celebrated, not regretted."

"I'm not alone. I have a big family, and there's Willie."

"Don't you want children, Matt? I saw you holding Barbie's baby. Don't you want a child of your own? Someone to share life with, to pass on the traditions of the McIntyres?" She wanted it for him. She wanted this good man to experience all the joys. He'd already had his share of the pain.

She saw a sudden hunger in his gaze as it dropped to her stomach.

"I'll have nieces and nephews aplenty, it appears," he said stiffly. "I don't have to have children for the McIntyres to continue."

She turned her back on him, crossing her arms over her stomach. "True."

Suddenly his arms surrounded her, and he whispered in her ear. "Thanks for wanting to…to help me, Elizabeth, but I'm fine. And interfering in someone's life isn't what you should do."

She couldn't believe his words. From Matt? She

whirled out of his hold. "You fraud! You've inter-
fered in my life from the day I met you. Now when
I try to do the same, you tell me it's not what I
should do?"

He grinned. "I wasn't trying to arrange your future. I was trying to protect you. That's different."

She rolled her eyes but figured she should cut her
losses. "I won't encourage anyone to marry you
off again. You're too ornery for any woman to put
up with, anyway." When she tried to skirt past him
to the door, however, he stopped her.

"I appreciate that, Elizabeth, but some women
think I'm an excellent catch."

Ah, she'd hurt his ego. "Perhaps you should find
one of those women. Then you could have an entire
tribe of McIntyres, and I'd have a good paying customer."

"So maybe I will," he returned, his blue eyes
flashing. But he didn't let her pass. Instead, he
pulled her against him and covered her lips with
his.

Not a gentle kiss. He demanded her attention, his
mouth seeking her cooperation.

She gave it, whether she wanted to or not. Something in her, in spite of her warnings to herself,
opened up to this man whenever he touched her.

When he finally released her, she was breathing
heavily. She was pleased to discover she wasn't the
only one affected when he drew a ragged breath.

"Just practicing," he muttered, a challenging
look on his handsome face.

Determined not to let him know how much the

kiss had devastated her, she tipped up her chin and said coolly, ''Good idea. I think your technique could use a little work.'' Then she escaped to the kitchen before the gathering storm on his face could erupt.

BAILEY AND JEFF RETURNED from New York in the middle of the week, happier than they'd ever been. She came to Elizabeth for a checkup, detailing a scare she'd had in New York, thinking she'd gone into labor.

Afterward, Elizabeth said, ''The doctor was right, but I also think it's a warning. You need to take care, get lots of rest. Airplane travel is stressful.''

''I'm going home for a nap now,'' Bailey assured her. ''With all the organizing you've been doing, I don't have that much work to do anymore. I'm going to start a new blanket for our baby. Oh! I didn't tell you. We're having a boy!''

''But you said it was a girl,'' Elizabeth pointed out.

Bailey shrugged. ''The doctor said the early screenings can sometimes be inaccurate.''

Elizabeth nodded. ''And he's in good health, as far as I can tell.''

''You'll be at the shower on Saturday?''

Elizabeth nodded again. ''Of course. Josie is having a lot of fun getting ready for it.''

''I worried about her doing too much. I mean, Annie has cut back on her work. You've even shortened your hours. But Josie tries to do everything.''

Elizabeth remembered Sunday dinner and the revelation about Justin's underwear. With a grin she said, ''Not everything, but I'm keeping an eye on her. With some of the relief she's gotten from managing the Millennium Baby Contest, I think she'll be all right.''

Bailey was her last appointment for the day. Since she was meeting Annie and Josie for lunch at Nell's, she invited her to join them.

Nell herself came to wait on them, bearing four glasses of milk. ''Here you go, ladies.''

''How did you know what we wanted?'' Josie teased.

''It's what you need,'' Nell told her firmly. Then she looked at Elizabeth. ''Matt was in earlier. He said you told him it was your fault.''

''Well, that's the truth. I appreciate your trying.''

''No problem.'' She took their orders and hurried to the kitchen.

''What was that all about?'' Bailey asked.

Josie made the explanation.

Elizabeth said nothing. She didn't want to think about the conversation she'd had with Matt last Sunday. Or the kiss he'd given her. And the hours of sleep she'd lost thinking about it.

That kiss had made her crave his touch even more. The man was driving her crazy.

''Are you worried about what happened?'' Josie asked.

Elizabeth snapped her head up. "No, of course not. I apologized."

"We told Elizabeth we picked her for Matt," Annie said with a smile.

"Perfect!" Bailey exclaimed.

Elizabeth just shook her head. She wasn't going to argue such a ridiculous idea again. Instead, she'd avoid all the McIntyres and their pregnant women. That would be best. Until Saturday, that is.

MATT, JUSTIN AND JEFF were having coffee in Jeff's apartment at The Way Station, waiting for Bailey's shower to be over. Then they'd transfer all the gifts upstairs.

"Glad you got that elevator put in," Matt said, taking a sip of his coffee. "It's going to make our job a lot easier. Otherwise we'd be climbing those stairs until dark."

"Yeah, and I don't have to worry about Bailey on the stairs now," Jeff added.

"Isn't it about time for them to be done?" Justin asked. "I have some things to do for the paper and—"

The phone interrupted them. Jeff answered it. His facial expression alerted the others to something out of the ordinary. Then he headed to the door, carrying the portable phone.

Matt and Justin hurried after him.

Bailey took the call when Jeff insisted. "Can you believe it? They want to put the contest on *The Oprah Winfrey Show*." Bailey couldn't contain her excitement.

Jeff suddenly stopped being a celebrant and turned to Bailey. "You don't mean you'll go back to New York? No way. It was too hard on you the last time. Elizabeth? Tell her she can't do that."

Matt watched Elizabeth. What would she say? She wouldn't compromise her care of her patients. He knew that much.

"It's only Chicago, I believe, but it's still not a trip I would recommend for any of my patients at this stage. Must we go to their studio? Can't they have us on the program long-distance?"

Everyone immediately latched on to that solution. Jeff put in a call to the television station in Casper, asking them if they could handle such a setup. Then Bailey called the lady she'd just talked to.

The television show would prefer a live presentation, but in the circumstances, they agreed to do a feed-in from Casper. When it was all arranged for the following Friday, everyone cheered.

"Just think of the money we're going to make!" Josie said, rubbing her hands together.

"I swear," Justin said with a grin, "she counts dollars in her sleep."

"But we're going to be able to buy our own ultrasound machine, Justin," Elizabeth reminded him. "And the hospital is going to be state-of-the-art. And it's all due to Josie, Annie and Bailey. It's incredible."

"You're doing your part, too," Matt added.

She smiled but shook her head.

"I'm going with you," Jeff said, distracting

everyone. "I'm not letting you fly down there by yourself."

"It's only a forty-minute flight, Jeff," Bailey said. "You've got things to do here."

"I'm going."

"Me, too," Justin added. When Josie opened her mouth, Matt assumed in protest, Justin added, "It's part of my job. I'll be covering it for the paper."

"Good. I want you to go," were her only words, and the two beamed at each other.

Matt wanted to go, too. He wanted to be there for Elizabeth. But while he'd told her he'd adopted her, he wasn't sure the rest of Bison City would understand. He didn't want to make things awkward for her.

"So we'll need reservations for six of us," Josie said, making a note. "And we'll have to discuss what we're wearing," she added, looking at her friends. "We don't want to clash."

Jeff moaned. "I think that means it's time for us to carry everything upstairs. I don't want to listen to a recitation of your wardrobes."

All the ladies laughed. Then there was a breaking up of the party. Everyone was anxious to spread the word about Bison City's notoriety.

The men, along with help from several of Jeff's employees, began loading their arms with boxes. As they rode upstairs in the elevator, Matt said, "You'll keep an eye on Elizabeth and Annie, too, won't you, guys?"

The other two stared at him, affronted looks on their faces.

"Of course we will," Jeff said indignantly.

"Annie's almost family," Justin added, "and Elizabeth is going to deliver our babies. We promise to bring them all back in one piece."

"Good." That was all he could say. And all he could do. Much to his regret.

Things changed early Friday morning.

The phone rang a little after six, just before he left the house. He and Willie exchanged alarmed looks and he raced for the phone.

"Hello?"

"Matt, it's Jeff. Can you go with the girls to Casper?"

"Sure. What's the problem?"

"There was a fire."

"At The Way Station? Is everyone all right?"

"Yeah. But it messed up three rooms, and we've got a full house this weekend. There's a lot to be done. Bailey said they could manage in Casper without me, but I'd feel better if you went along, too. I don't want to overload Justin."

"I'm happy to go. What time are they leaving?"

"The flight takes off at nine. We were going to pick everyone up at seven forty-five. You'd better use our Suburban."

Matt agreed. He couldn't fit everyone into his pickup. He hung up the phone and explained the situation to Willie. "I'm going to go talk to the foreman, then I'll be back to change clothes. See if my navy suit is okay and find me a tie that looks good."

He hurried out without waiting for an answer.

When the plane left the gate at nine, he was strapped into the seat next to Elizabeth, a smile on his face.

"How's Sarah Beth this morning?" Matt asked, leaning toward Elizabeth, drawing in her scent.

"I think she's still asleep," Elizabeth said, her hazel eyes half-closed. "I wish I was."

The plane hit a bump as it rolled down the landing strip. Elizabeth gripped the armrest until her knuckles turned white.

"Are you a nervous flyer?" he asked, prying one hand off the rest and enveloping it with his own.

"N-not usually. But I think we hit something."

"Nope," he assured her. "At least, nothing important. It was probably a clod of dirt under the snow." He squeezed her hand, glad he was with her. "Don't worry. I won't let anything hurt you."

Chapter Twelve

Since they weren't doing the interview live, the people at the television station explained everything to the four women and gave them plenty of time to prepare.

Matt and Justin stood behind the cameras, watching the Bison City ladies settle down for the recording. Just as they were about to start, Elizabeth waved frantically.

Matt was at her side in two seconds. "What is it, sweetheart? Are you sick?"

"Tissue!" she gasped, covering her face.

Fortunately one of the assistants ran forward with the requisite tissue. Elizabeth grabbed it just before she sneezed.

"Damn it, you gave me a heart attack," Matt muttered. When she glared at him, he hugged her and kissed her cheek before he backed away again.

The connection to the hostess of the talk show had already been established.

"Are you okay?" Oprah asked.

"Oh, yes. I'm sorry. Did I mess it all up?" Elizabeth asked anxiously.

"Not at all. They'll cut the sneeze out. Now, let's get to the good stuff. How many ladies in Bison City are pregnant?"

After numerous questions, which each of the four women took turns answering, Oprah asked an unexpected question. "Who's that hunk who was helping you earlier, Elizabeth?"

Matt froze. He hadn't realized he'd been on camera.

"That was Matt McIntyre, Josie's brother."

"And is Bison City full of men like him?"

They all looked at each other, then nodded yes.

"Bring him back on camera," Oprah ordered.

"My husband is here, too," Josie said even as Justin was shaking his head no. She motioned for him to join her.

Both men had to be prodded by station employees. When they were standing behind the seated women, Oprah gave them her full attention.

"My, my, my. Now I understand why all those women are pregnant. They sure grow them handsome in Bison City. Which one of you is Josie's husband?"

Justin, standing with his hands on Josie's shoulders, nodded.

"Ah, Mr. Talkative. What do you do for a living?"

"I'm the mayor of Bison City and the owner and editor of the *Bison City Bugle*."

Oprah congratulated him and turned to Matt. "So you're Josie's brother?"

He nodded.

"And which baby are you responsible for?"

"All of them," he said.

There was stunned silence, then a babble of protests, while Oprah reared back in her chair in laughter.

"I didn't mean that the way it came out. I meant I'm responsible for taking care of all of them," Matt tried to explain. "Three of these babies are part of my family."

"Which one isn't?" Oprah asked as she wiped a tear from her eye.

"Elizabeth's baby. She's a widow. And a good friend." He squeezed her shoulders as he added the last. The urge to claim her baby as his own had almost pushed him into saying something else inappropriate.

"Well, I'm relieved to know you haven't been populating Bison City on your own. Do you have any children?"

"No, ma'am, I don't."

"Okay, well, thanks for the visit, ladies. Tell our viewers how they can order the calendar or enter the sweepstakes."

Bailey gave the prices and the address. Then the director yelled, "Clear."

Matt knew his cheeks were hot. He'd felt hot earlier, but he'd blamed it on the television lights. He couldn't do that now.

"Josie, I'm sorry I messed up," he said.

The director answered before Josie could. "You probably helped them instead of hurting them."

Everyone stared at him. "You made Oprah laugh. Humor sells. Otherwise, she might've cut the segment short. I bet you get the full ten minutes we put on tape."

Everyone else was excited about what he'd said, but Matt wasn't. "Well, I'm glad my embarrassment wasn't a total loss."

Elizabeth took his hand in hers as she stood. "Don't worry about it, Matt. It's your fifteen minutes of fame. No one will even remember it next week."

"Thanks," he muttered, wondering why the room seemed to be wavering. "Are we having an earthquake?" he asked.

"Matt? Matt, what's wrong?" Elizabeth asked urgently.

He couldn't answer. With a groan, he folded over.

ELIZABETH BROKE HIS FALL, but fortunately Justin grabbed hold of Matt, taking most of his weight.

"What's wrong?" Josie demanded.

Elizabeth had already felt his face and was taking his pulse. "He's got a fever. We need to get him to the hospital."

The car that had picked them up at the airport was brought around and they made a fast trip to the hospital. Elizabeth consulted with the emergency room doctor and discovered, as she'd suspected, that Matt was suffering from a flu that had been making its way up from Texas. Dave had mentioned several cases the past week.

She sent the others off to have lunch, while she remained with Matt. He was receiving an IV.

"What's going on? Why am I in this bed?" he demanded groggily.

"You've got the flu," the E.R. doctor told him. "We're giving you some fluid. Then you should be able to make it back home. A couple of days in bed, and you'll be back to normal."

"Get her out of here!" Matt suddenly yelled.

The doctor stared at first Matt and then Elizabeth. Thankfully she had time to compose her features, hiding the hurt Matt's brusque dismissal caused her.

The doctor said calmly, "Dr. Lee is a qualified physician, Mr. McIntyre."

"I know that," he said faintly, "but she's pregnant. I don't want her or the baby to get sick." Then he closed his eyes.

"I'll take every precaution," she assured the doctor, "but I've already been exposed. We traveled down together."

"Well, as long as you didn't touch him, there's probably no problem. Germs don't leap around."

Elizabeth tried to keep from blushing, but her thoughts dwelled on his warm hand holding hers, offering reassurance. She certainly wasn't going to turn away when he needed her.

"Ah. I see. Is he the father of your baby?" the doctor asked.

Elizabeth glared at him. "The father of my child

is none of your business," she informed him glacially.

"No, of course not," the man said, backing toward the door. "Absolutely not. I…I have other patients to see."

And he disappeared.

"Way to go, Elizabeth," she muttered. "You managed to offend a nice man who asked a reasonable question."

"'Lizabeth?" Matt muttered.

She hurried to his bedside.

"Are we alone?"

"Yes."

He reached out blindly, and she took his hand.

"'Lizabeth? I want to be Sarah Beth's daddy."

Her heart lurched and she almost lost her balance. Then it settled back into place. Matt had found a replacement for his lost child. Hers. He didn't mean he wanted *her*. He just wanted her baby.

"Get some rest, Matt," she said firmly. "I'll be back in a little while."

"'Lizabeth?" he called as she left the room. But she didn't return to his side.

MATT FELT LIKE A FOOL. At least he'd been able to walk out of the hospital on his own two feet. At quite a distance from Elizabeth.

He'd made an even greater fool of himself when he'd asked to be Sarah Beth's daddy. Elizabeth didn't want him. She couldn't have made it clearer. Oh, she hadn't given him the big rejection.

Not when he was lying helpless in a hospital bed.

But she gave her answer every time she avoided his gaze, his touch, his presence. He should've waited until he was on his feet, strong again. Until he could take her into his arms and convince her.

Maybe he should even have waited until after Sarah Beth came into the world.

But he hadn't wanted to wait. He'd wanted to welcome Sarah Beth as his own. Just as he wanted to hold Elizabeth in his arms, protected from the world, a part of him.

As Julie had been. He'd loved his wife. How their marriage would've grown, he didn't know. He hadn't been given the chance to know.

He'd never expected to love again.

But Elizabeth, with her strength, her independence, her determination to give her best to her baby, drew him from his lonely world. Her soft lips, slender frame, big heart, all made him long to hold her close.

He couldn't believe the way things had turned out.

When they entered the small plane to fly back to Bison City, he discovered himself sitting beside Bailey. Elizabeth was in front of him, seated with Annie.

She might as well have been a million miles away.

When he got out of the plane, Elizabeth was talking to Justin. Then she walked away.

"Elizabeth?" he called.

Justin stepped forward. "Elizabeth said I should take you to Dr. Dave."

"Where's she going?"

"She said she was going to take Charlie's taxi home before she came to the hospital. She called home while you were in bed and discovered you're not the only case to break out."

"But she shouldn't be exposing herself to the germs!" Matt protested, growing more frantic.

"Easy, buddy, easy," Justin cautioned. "Let's get the ladies back home. Then we'll check in with Dave, just to be on the safe side. You'll probably see Elizabeth there."

Matt didn't argue. He was feeling too miserable for a lot of reasons. But he wasn't surprised when he didn't catch a glimpse of Elizabeth, much less get to talk to her.

Justin drove him home in Jeff's Suburban.

Dave had warned him not to drive. And to go straight to bed. "You'll be over it in forty-eight hours, I promise, even if you don't feel like it now."

Matt groaned as Justin hit a bump.

"Sorry. You feeling worse?"

"I've felt better," Matt muttered, leaning his head against the side of the vehicle.

When Justin stopped the truck near the back porch, he hurried around it to help Matt out. He'd told Josie to let Willie know she had a patient coming home. She met them on the back porch, reaching an arm around Matt.

"Mercy, he's as white as a sheet," she said to Justin.

"Doc said this hits hard and fast. His medicine is in his coat pocket. He's due for another pill in an hour. And Doc said to push fluids, juice especially."

"'Course. I've got plenty on hand. And some broth, too. Got to keep his strength up."

"I can still talk," Matt protested, hating how weak his voice sounded. "You're acting like I've already passed out."

"Come on, boy," Willie ordered, pushing him ahead of her up the stairs, ignoring his protest.

When they entered the bedroom, she ordered, "Get out of those clothes."

Matt wasn't so far gone that he'd strip in front of his housekeeper. "Leave the room first."

"I've seen a man in his underwear before," she assured him.

"Maybe so, but not today. Justin will help me."

Willie frowned but turned and left the room.

"Way to go, Matt. I thought she'd refuse."

"Me, too," Matt said with a sigh and slumped to the bed.

ELIZABETH WORRIED about Matt, but she didn't see him. She did, however, check with Dave for an update. That was about all she had time for. It was as if the flu struck everyone at the same time.

Her shortened hours went by the wayside, especially when she was consulting with Dave four days later and noticed his flushed face. "Dave, are you running a fever?"

He shrugged. "Maybe a low-grade one. Nothing to worry about."

She immediately called Evelyn in. "Take his temperature," she ordered briskly. "Have you been wearing a mask, like we talked about?"

"I forgot," he muttered.

"Oh, dear," Elizabeth muttered, when Evelyn showed her the register on the thermometer. "Dave, your temperature is 101. You've got the flu."

She immediately administered what care she could give him. Then she had one of the nurses take him home.

"Well," she muttered to herself. She'd tried to wear herself out each day so she'd sleep without giving any thought to the big, stubborn man she loved. Who loved her baby. Now she wouldn't have any difficulty with that plan. She was responsible for the entire town's health. She put in a call to the next city for any help they could give her, but they, too, were experiencing a wave of influenza.

Friday morning she realized with a sigh of relief the crisis had passed. The waiting room had only a couple of people when she arrived. She had a relaxing morning, with no emergencies.

"I think we're okay, ladies," she told her nurses. "Thanks for all your help."

By two o'clock she'd decided to go home early. She hadn't been feeling too well herself, though it wasn't the flu. She thought Sarah Beth was protesting the long hours.

Just as she was preparing to leave, the phone rang.

Evelyn answered it, then quickly handed the receiver to Elizabeth. "Hello? This is Dr. Elizabeth. Can I help you?"

"I...I can't—" a rusty voice cried. "Help me."

"Yes, I'll help you. Who is this?"

"Dan...Dan Martin—"

Then she heard the receiver crash to the floor. "Mr. Martin? Mr. Martin?"

No response.

"Do either of you know a Dan Martin?" she asked the nurses.

"Sure," Evelyn said. "He's old, probably in his eighties. Lives alone about half an hour from town."

"He's passed out. I'll go to him. Can you write down directions?"

"I'll go with you," Evelyn immediately said.

"No. I promised Alice she could go to her son's Christmas party at school, remember? I'll need you to keep the office open."

"I can miss it," Alice volunteered.

"No, it's not necessary. Just draw me a good map."

She went back into her office to gather what she thought she'd need. Then she picked up the map, studying it quickly. With a thank-you, she was on her way, hoping and praying she wasn't too late.

MATT STUDIED THE SKIES. Then he pulled his cellular phone out of his pocket. "Willie? What's the weather say?''

''I haven't checked since noon, Matt. That storm was supposed to come in late tonight. Just a minute.''

He heard the radio come on. She was back on the line a minute later. ''They've changed the forecast. The storm is moving fast and it's big. It'll probably be here around three. You'd better get everybody in.''

''Right.'' He'd already been making preparations for the storm. It didn't take long to spread the word. The first flakes began falling about two-thirty. Big, beautiful flakes that coated the ground in half an hour.

When he reached the house, after rubbing down his horse and storing his tack, there was already an inch of snow on the ground, and it was coming down faster and faster.

He gratefully entered the kitchen, heading for the coffeepot automatically.

''Good thing you got here,'' Willie commented. ''It's getting bad out there already.''

''Yeah.'' He sipped the coffee, staring out the window over the kitchen sink.

Abruptly he set down the cup and strode to the phone. Ever since the trip to Casper, he'd tried to stop thinking about Elizabeth, to stop hoping for a future with her.

But that didn't mean he should stop protecting her.

When there was no answer at her home, he called the hospital. "Is Dr. Elizabeth there?"

"No. Do you have an emergency?"

"Evelyn, is that you? This is Matt McIntyre. I just wanted to be sure Elizabeth wasn't out in this weather."

"Oh, Matt, I'm so glad you called. I don't know what to do."

"What is it?" he demanded, a sick feeling in his stomach.

"Dan Martin called, and then he passed out. Dr. Elizabeth went out to his place to help him. She called over an hour ago. He died."

"I'm sorry. Where is she now?"

"That's just it. She was coming back here, but she should be here by now...and I haven't heard from her."

Matt could see the snow coming down from where he stood. Panic built in him. "I'm going to find her. You stay there in case I need help with her."

"Yes, sir. Please find her."

"I will," he promised.

He got off the phone and turned to Willie. "Pack me some coffee, soup, anything hot you've got. Elizabeth went to Dan Martin's. He died. And she hasn't come back."

"Mercy!" Willie said with a gasp, and immediately sprang to action.

Matt rushed up the stairs and gathered several thermal blankets. In the laundry room he found a plastic tarp that would shield them from the snow.

When he reached the kitchen again, he discovered Willie had a box of food waiting for him.

"Good luck," she whispered as he hugged her. Then he picked up the box and headed to the barn where he'd parked his truck.

Dan Martin's place was on the other side of Bison City. On a normal day it would take twenty-five minutes. But with the snow, he'd be lucky to make it in twice that time.

He couldn't believe the woman he loved was at risk because of a winter storm—again. This time, though, he wouldn't fail. This time, he'd save Elizabeth and the baby. This time.

He almost spun out as he took a corner too fast. Realizing he'd do Elizabeth no good if he didn't get there, he slowed down. But only a little.

The cold was vicious. Even if she hadn't had a wreck, if she was exposed to the elements for long, she might be beyond his help.

He hit a long stretch of road and pressed down on the accelerator again. He couldn't see far, but he knew the road well. So well, that he was past the car that had slid into the ditch before he reacted. Braking, he came to a halt and threw the truck into reverse.

He prayed Elizabeth had stayed in the car.

Chapter Thirteen

Snow covering the windows made it impossible to see if anyone was in the car. His heart in his throat, Matt slid into the ditch and swiped at the windshield.

A pale, frightened face stared back at him. With a prayer of gratitude, he sprang to the driver's door. It was locked. He banged on the window.

Elizabeth unlocked the door and almost fell into Matt's arms as he opened it.

"Matt! I was so frightened. I'm stuck."

"I know. Come on." He didn't waste breath on any more conversation. There wasn't time. With his arms wrapped around her, he pushed them both back up to the road and to his truck.

Shoving Elizabeth in on the passenger side, he grabbed the two thermal blankets and wrapped them around her.

"M-m-my bag," she whispered.

With a muttered curse, he closed her door and slid back into the ditch to retrieve her bag from the back seat. Then he climbed to the road again, this time going to the driver's side.

"Are you warming up?" he asked as he slid behind the wheel. "Can you feel your fingers and toes?"

"Y-y-yes. Thank you, Matt. I…I thought I was going to freeze to death."

Before he started driving, he reached in the box on the seat between them and took out the thermos. Pouring coffee into the foam cup Willie had provided, he handed it to Elizabeth.

Her hand was too shaky. He kept his wrapped around the cup and guided it to her lips. "I know you don't normally drink coffee but you need something hot inside you."

"Oh, y-yes," she said in a whisper and sipped the hot liquid. After several drinks she leaned back against the seat.

Matt drank a little coffee, then handed the cup back to Elizabeth. "Hold it. It'll warm your hands."

He cautiously backed his truck until he found a place to turn around. Then he drove slowly back the way he'd come. The storm was still intensifying, and he could barely see the hood of his truck, much less the road.

He considered their options. He didn't think they'd be able to get back home until the storm died down, and that depended on the amount of snow that fell. Staying in the truck wasn't a good option, either.

So he had to find shelter. Mentally he reviewed

the road. He remembered a small cabin a couple of miles away. He was pretty sure it belonged to some snowbirds, a retired couple who moved south every October, returning in May to spend the summer in Wyoming. It wouldn't be great, but it would give them some shelter.

Slowly he inched the truck forward, trying to stay on the road, though he was having trouble seeing it. He barely caught the outline of the cabin when he reached it. Fortunately, it sat close to the road, or he would've passed it by.

He glanced over at Elizabeth. Even her face was buried in the blankets. Had she gone to sleep? "Elizabeth?"

"Yes?" she responded, raising her gaze to his. She wore a dazed look, as if exhausted.

"I'm going to check out this cabin. You stay put until I come back for you."

Fear washed over her features, but she didn't protest. "Be careful."

He nodded and slipped out into the storm.

ELIZABETH LOST SIGHT of him at once. She was alone again in the storm. But this time she had heat and coffee and Matt's promise to return.

She clung to that promise, straining to see into the storm, to find any sign that he'd kept his promise. When he suddenly appeared at the window of the truck, she trembled in relief.

He swung open the door, then scooped her into his arms. Even with his big body shielding her, the storm beat against her, the cold taking instant hold of her body. She buried her face against Matt's neck and held on for dear life.

It took a minute for her to realize the storm was no longer around her. Matt was still moving. She opened her eyes to discover they were inside a house.

"Where are we?" she whispered.

"It's a cabin used during the summer. We're going to borrow it." Matt laid her down on a bed in one corner. "I'll be back in a minute."

He'd left her again. The panic attack that followed his disappearance was absurd, she assured herself, as was the belief that all would be well whenever he appeared. But she couldn't help herself.

He burst back into the cabin almost immediately, carrying the box from the truck, as well as her medical bag.

"Hang on, Elizabeth. I'll start a fire."

For the first time she noticed an old-fashioned potbellied stove in the opposite corner from the bed. Matt disappeared out the door again, then returned, carrying wood. He made several trips, dumping his load down near the fire each time.

She should help. He was doing all the work. When she made a move to rise from the bed, however, Matt said sharply, "Stay down."

"I could help," she offered.

"No. I want you to stay under those blankets. It's below freezing in here."

So she watched him as he started a fire, using some paper toweling the owners had left on the counter. The greedy little flame was encouraging. As he laid several pieces of wood into the stove, Elizabeth began to relax.

She must've drifted off for a minute or two. When she opened her eyes, Matt was at the door, taping something.

"What are you doing?"

He looked over his shoulder. "Trying to block the storm from coming in. I had to break the window pane to get in."

"Will you get in trouble?" she asked, anxiously.

He turned his surprised gaze on her. "In trouble? Nope. Besides, I'll have it repaired before the owners ever return. In Wyoming you have to take shelter wherever you can find it during these winter storms."

He stepped back and studied his handiwork. "That should hold." Then he turned to the box he'd carried in. "Willie packed some food. Are you hungry?"

"Yes, I missed lunch."

"That's not good for Sarah Beth."

"It's not good for me, either, but I intended to go home early today, for the first time this week. I thought I'd eat then."

"A rough week?" he asked with his back to her.

In so many ways. The fact that she'd had to avoid him had made it the worst week in a long time. "There were a lot of sick people."

"At least you had Dave to share the load."

"He went down with the flu on Wednesday."

Matt whirled around. "You've been managing on your own?"

"There was no one else." She watched as his gaze flared with anger.

"Damn it, Elizabeth! You should've called for help from somewhere!"

"I tried. Everyone was experiencing the same problem. And don't yell at me," she added in a whisper that revealed how tired she was.

Matt crossed the room and scooped her up into his arms again. He buried his face in her hair and muttered, "Sorry." She didn't fight the surge of feelings that filled her. She'd longed for his touch, his concern, the past week. Life without Matt was lonely.

Then he stood, lifting her, and crossed back to the stove and the rough table and chairs that sat near it.

He set her down in the chair closest to the fire. "Are you warm enough?"

She was still wrapped in the two blankets, and the heat from the stove was making the air in the room a little less frigid. But the loss of his arms around her superseded the heat from the stove.

"I'm fine," she muttered.

He turned his attention back to the food. Putting several sandwiches, wrapped in plastic bags, on the table, he added two more foam cups and began pouring coffee in the first one.

"Could I have water?" she asked.

"Are you sure? I want you warmed up inside and out."

"I'm sure."

"It will have to be melted snow. They don't have running water in here." He opened a lower cabinet and found a pan. Then he moved to the door. Though he stepped outside quickly and pulled the door to, a blast of cold air blew through the room. In seconds he reversed the procedure.

She hadn't moved, her attention fixed on him.

He put the pan on top of the stove. "It shouldn't take long to melt," he assured her. Then he sat down at the table. "Aren't you going to eat your sandwich?"

"Yes, of course. It was good of Willie to fix them for us." She opened a plastic bag and took out the roast beef sandwich. With Matt's gaze on her, she self-consciously took a bite.

As if her eating was a signal, he began eating. No conversation took place, which was a relief. She hadn't spoken to him since they'd been in the hospital in Casper. When he asked to be Sarah Beth's daddy.

"You didn't get the flu?" he asked suddenly.

"No. Neither did Josie, Bailey or Annie."

"Yeah, I heard."

"The *Oprah* show was supposed to be on television today." She'd set her VCR to record it.

Matt groaned. "If she kept my part in it, I won't be able to face anyone again."

Elizabeth couldn't hold back a smile. "It provided some humor, you'll have to admit."

"Yeah."

She switched to another topic, one that had been

uppermost on her mind the past half hour. "Matt, thank you for coming to look for me today."

He didn't say anything.

"Or did you just happen along that road?"

"No. I came looking for you."

"I would've died if you hadn't," she said softly, her eyes filling with tears.

He stared at her, then dropped his gaze back to the sandwich in his hand. "You're safe now."

"Yes. How long will we have to stay here?"

He looked toward the one window near the bed. Then he shrugged his shoulders. "Depends on the storm. It's fierce, but it was supposed to be short. We'll probably be able to leave in the morning."

She nodded and tried to casually check her watch. It was only a little after five. They were going to spend a lot of time together. Nervously, she said, "T-too bad we don't have a television and some movies to watch. I've missed a lot of the movies that came out this year because I didn't have time to see them. Now I've got time and no movies."

"You like movies?" he asked.

"Yes. They help me relax. Don't you like movies?"

"Don't see many of them unless they come on television. It's too much trouble to rent them. I forget to return them and the rental people get upset."

"I guess they would."

"Yeah."

Her baby stirred and Elizabeth rubbed her stomach. She was feeling some discomfort even when Sarah Beth was still, and that worried her.

"Everything all right?" Matt asked, his gaze sharp.

"Yes, of course," she assured him, smoothing the frown away. It wouldn't do any good for both of them to worry. She just needed rest. The workload this week had taken a lot out of her. That was it. She needed rest.

He stood abruptly and crossed to the stove. After checking the pan, he filled her foam cup with water. "If it's too warm, it'll cool quickly."

"Yes, thank you." The water was barely warm and she drank it, grateful for the liquid.

"Finish your sandwich," he ordered as he sat down again. "When it's cold, you need lots of calories to heat your body."

"I'm not sure that's a proven scientific fact," she said doubtfully.

"Then eat because I don't know when we'll get our next meal," he said with a smile.

"I'm not really hungry anymore. I'll save this half of the sandwich and we can share it later."

"Your appetite still off?" he asked.

She'd forgotten she'd mentioned her dwindling appetite. "Yes, I guess so."

WITH A LONG EVENING in front of them, Matt scanned the little cabin for a distraction. There were a few books on a nearby shelf, but it was already growing dark. Reading would be difficult.

He got up to look for candles. He found several

in one of the cabinets. And something to pass the time.

"What kind of card games can you play?" he asked.

Elizabeth looked up in surprise, her hazel eyes wide. "Card games?"

"I found a deck of cards. It'll help pass the time."

"Will we be able to see well enough to play?"

"Just call me Robinson Crusoe. I found candles." He set two in the small star-shaped holders and brought them to the table, along with the cards. He pulled out the lighter he'd found earlier to use on the fire and lit the candles. "Still cold?" he asked.

"Not anymore. Even my toes are thawed out," she assured him.

Matt relaxed a little more. He'd been so afraid he'd lose her and her baby. Until he had her home safe, he wouldn't completely relax, but at least she was warm now.

"So, do you play gin?" he asked.

Several hours later they'd played every game they both knew. Elizabeth had beaten him at gin. He'd taken her when they played poker. Neither had done well at Honeymoon Spades.

Matt decided they'd played enough. "Maybe we'd better call it a night. We're both tired."

After a brief trip outside, Matt waited for Elizabeth to return also.

The door opened and closed and Elizabeth ran to the stove. "I...I...I don't expect my rear to thaw out until next summer,'' she muttered, placing that part of her anatomy closest to the stove.

"We don't have much more wood, do we?" she asked him.

He glanced down at the dwindling pile beside the stove. "No, there's not a lot left."

He cleared his throat. Here came the hard part. Time to clarify their situation. "There's only one bed, Elizabeth."

She nodded, staring at him.

"Even if we had another bed, we'd have to share. We're going to need each other's body heat to stay warm. We need to save as much wood as we can in case it's still storming tomorrow."

He watched her stare at the bed, waited for her protests. Then, after licking her lips, she stood, saying, "Okay."

He rose, reaching out to caress her cheek. "I promise it's necessary."

"I know."

"We'll need to use the two blankets. And I'll spread the plastic tarp on top of those. It'll help insulate us. You want to get in bed first?"

She nodded and crossed the small room. "Should I keep on my coat?"

"No, we'll be better off if we take off our coats and shoes. But keep on your cap. It will help hold the heat in."

She peeled off her coat and slipped out of her shoes.

"Uh, you should loosen anything that's too

tight," he added, looking away from her rounded form.

"You mean my bra?" she asked and he discovered she was smiling at him. "It's okay, it's not tight."

He nodded. He added another piece of wood to the stove, figuring he'd have to get up several times during the night to add wood.

After Elizabeth had lain down on the bed, he spread the two blankets over her, leaving room for him. Then he took the plastic tarp he'd brought with him and put it on top.

Sitting down, he pulled off his boots and his coat. Then, drawing a deep breath, he blew out the candles and rose to cross to the bed. Elizabeth had her eyes closed, as if she expected him to disrobe.

He lifted the covers and slid underneath, immediately feeling the heat from her body. Heat that he craved. Afraid he'd scare her, he stretched out beside her, careful not to touch her.

They lay in stiff silence for several minutes.

"Matt?" Elizabeth whispered.

"Yeah?"

"I'm still cold."

With a sigh of relief, he reached out for her, wrapping an arm around her. As naturally as if she'd slept with him all her life, she slipped her head on his shoulder and snuggled against him.

"Better?"

"Mmm-hmm," she said, her voice drowsy.

Matt rested his other hand on Elizabeth's hip, cradling her against him, offering a prayer of thanks that he'd found her in the storm, that he could hold her through the night.

Sarah Beth beat a tattoo in her mother's tummy, pressed against his. He chuckled. "I think Sarah Beth's waking up," he whispered.

He slid his hand beneath Elizabeth's maternity top to rub her stomach. When his hand connected with her warm flesh, she gasped.

"Is my hand too cold?" he asked.

"No," she whispered, her hand covering his to hold it against her stomach. "I think Sarah Beth likes it."

"She's not the only one," he whispered in return.

When she raised her gaze to his face, he covered her lips with his, kissing her as he'd longed to do, as a lover reunited with his lost love. She didn't pull away. Instead, she opened her mouth to his, mingling her breath with his, her warmth with his warmth.

He ran his hands over her body, wanting to know her, to claim her as his own. When a foal was born, horse trainers did the same thing. They called it imprinting. From then on the animal belonged to the trainer, always recognizing his scent, his touch.

Matt wanted Elizabeth, and Sarah Beth, too, to know his touch, to belong to him. And for him to belong to them. A deep ache, a recognition of his loneliness, filled him. But with Elizabeth in his arms, he felt fulfilled.

Their kisses intensified as they each tried to get closer, deeper, to become one, to know the ultimate oneness. Her clothes were in his way, and Matt began to slide her long pants down her silken body.

"No! No, Matt, we can't. The baby—" She broke off on a sob. "I'm sorry. I know I shouldn't have—"

With a groan, he covered her lips again. But this time, he was consoling, nurturing, not trying to swallow her whole. "It's okay, Elizabeth. I wouldn't want to do anything that would hurt the baby," he whispered as he lifted his lips.

She touched his arousal, a fact he couldn't hide. "I didn't mean to lead you on," she whispered. "But I thought I was going to die today, and it felt so good to be alive. To be held. To be loved."

"It obviously felt good to me, too," he assured her with a chuckle.

"But what— Surely there are other…things we could do."

"I'll be fine. Just let me hold you," he added, not liking the distance between them.

"But won't it make your r-recovery more difficult?"

"Yeah. But it will be worth every minute of it."

At first hesitant, she finally settled against his body, letting him wrap his arms around her.

Okay, so maybe he'd have trouble getting to sleep. It was okay. She wouldn't always be pregnant. But she'd always be his. He was determined about that.

HE CAME AWAKE ABRUPTLY.

Immediately aware of Elizabeth pressed against

him, he didn't move, his mind trying to identify what had disturbed his sleep.

Then she stirred.

"Elizabeth? Are you awake?"

"Yes," she said in a small, fearful voice.

"What's wrong?"

"Matt, I...I think I'm in labor."

Chapter Fourteen

"But...but it's not time!" he protested, panic in his voice.

"I know," she said tearily.

"Are you sure?"

"No. But I haven't been feeling well. I thought it was because I was tired."

"We didn't— I mean, last night didn't—"

"No!" she returned, her face flushed.

Relief filled his face. "What can I do?" he asked.

"If...if I can get to the hospital, I can get a shot that might stop the labor, if it's not too advanced. But the storm..."

Matt reared his head. "Hear that? The storm has passed. The wind's hardly blowing. Wait here."

He slid from the bed, taking the heat with him. She watched him in the darkness. He crossed to the door and opened it. She could feel the cold, but he was right about the wind having died down.

"Has it stopped snowing?"

"Yeah, it has. We've got to try to make it to town."

"I'm not sure I'm in labor, Matt. It could be just a twinge," she warned, afraid she was panicking needlessly.

He looked at his watch. "It's a quarter to six. By the time we get there, the town will be stirring. I'll get my phone. You can call Dave and have him meet us there."

"But he's had the flu. I shouldn't disturb—"

"Either you call him or I will. You've carried the load for him the past few days. He can get up early for you."

He came back to the bed and held out the phone he'd taken from his coat.

She took it, frowning. "Why didn't you call anyone last night?"

"It wouldn't have gotten through in the blizzard. Do you know his number?"

"Yes, but—"

"Call." His hard command let her know he was serious.

Reluctantly she dialed her partner's number.

"Dave? I'm sorry to bother you but…but I think I may be in early labor. Could you meet me at the hospital?" Dave's immediate response reassured her somewhat. She looked at Matt. "He wants to know how long?"

"We'll be there in half an hour, or a little sooner."

She repeated his words, then disconnected. "He'll meet us there."

"Any more pains?"

"Not yet." She knew he could hear the fear in her voice, but she couldn't help it.

"I'm going out to warm up the truck. Do you need to go outside again?"

She shook her head.

"Then stay in bed until I get back."

She nodded her compliance. In fact, she scarcely breathed, hoping if she didn't move, Sarah Beth would forget her impatience to arrive.

"Just wait a few more weeks, little one. I promise it'll be for the best." She wanted her baby girl to have a good, safe start to life. Premature babies could have so many problems.

She'd expected to be embarrassed this morning, when she awoke. She'd taken advantage of Matt last night, seeking his comfort, his touch, when she knew they couldn't fully satisfy each other. But she'd needed him to hold her.

Now, however, she dismissed such thoughts. Sarah Beth's health was so much more important.

Matt opened the door. "It's not any warmer out there, but I think we can make it. Put on your coat and shoes. I'll tidy up here."

She did as he said, moving slowly, even though the cold air urged her to hurry. When she was finished, she discovered Matt at her side.

"I'm going to carry you to the truck. Just stand there a minute while I fold the blankets."

"I can—"

"No. Don't move."

Since his words only reiterated what she wanted,

she didn't even complain about his bossiness. In fact, following his orders was reassuring.

He carried the blankets to the truck, along with the box of provisions. When he came back, he swept her into his arms and retraced his steps. He already had the passenger door open.

She slid onto the seat. The blankets were on the floorboard, and the box was nowhere in sight. Before she could ask any questions, however, he closed the door and went back to shut up the cabin.

When he slid behind the wheel, she asked, "Where's the box?"

"In the back. Slide over here beside me."

She did as he asked. His warmth helped keep the cold away, but it also filled her with hope. Matt McIntyre was as good as any medicine at making her feel better.

"Okay, we're off. It won't be long now, Elizabeth. Just hold on."

"I'm doing fine, Matt. I haven't had another pain. I probably panicked. Dave will have gotten out of bed for nothing."

"We'll see," he said quietly, and concentrated on his driving.

She laid her head against his shoulder and closed her eyes. Time would pass faster that way, and she wouldn't have to see any near misses they might have.

About five minutes later she had another pain.

Matt knew at once. "Another one."

She nodded her head against his shoulder.

"Hang on tight, baby. We'll be there soon."

"Are you talking to me or Sarah Beth?" she asked, trying to smile.

"Whoever's listening," he whispered.

"They're far enough apart that I think the shot will work," she said softly, trying to encourage herself as well as Matt.

"Good. It must be worse on you than the other women because you know all that can go wrong," he said, reaching an arm around her to pull her more tightly against him.

"Don't you need your arm to drive?" she asked anxiously

"Naw. I practiced driving one-handed a lot when I was a teenager."

She chuckled, surprising herself. "I'll bet you did. You probably had a long line of volunteers to help you."

"A few," he returned, laughing a little.

She wished she'd known him then. She hoped Sarah Beth met someone like Matt when she was all grown. A good man.

The first buildings of the town came into sight. Elizabeth breathed a little easier. They'd be there soon. When she saw the hospital, the sight of Dave's car waiting in front was even more encouraging. "Dave's already there."

"Good." He parked beside the other vehicle. "I'm coming around to carry you. Don't move."

"I can walk," she protested, but she did as he said. She felt protected when he carried her. And she needed that feeling right now.

Dave held the door open, waiting for them. "Bring her this way," he ordered Matt.

Matt placed her on the examining table.

"If you'll step—" Dave began.

Matt took her hand. "Nope. I'm staying…unless you want me to go." He looked at her, a question in his blue eyes.

"You can stay," she whispered, tightening her hold on his hand. He stood beside her head, smiling at her, ignoring Dave while he examined her.

"I think we're in time," Dave said. "You haven't dilated all that much. I'll get the shot."

He left the room.

"Matt?"

"Yeah?"

"Thank you for staying with me. I know it's a lot to ask, but—"

"You're not the one who asked. I did." He bent over and brushed her lips with his.

He straightened as Dave returned, and grinned. "I hope you're braver about shots than I am."

His teasing made her feel better. "Are you a fainter?" she asked.

"Not quite, but I sure hate them."

Dave grinned. "Then I'll try not to get the wrong victim."

Matt watched him cautiously, as if he believed Dave could make that mistake.

Elizabeth grimaced as Dave injected the medicine, then took a deep breath. "It should take effect fairly soon."

"Hey, I'm the doctor here," Dave protested. "It

should take effect fairly soon," he added, repeating her words exactly. "Why did it take you so long to get here? I know the roads are bad, but you're only five minutes away."

"I wasn't at home." She related the events of yesterday.

"Damn it, Elizabeth!" Dave protested. "You should've called me. You had no business going out in a storm. You don't know how to drive on snow."

"I know. But Matt saved me." She squeezed his hand.

"My pleasure," he assured her, a crooked grin on his lips.

"Listen, I'm going to call one of the nurses to come take care of you. You'll have to stay overnight so we can keep you off your feet," Dave said.

He left the room before Elizabeth could think. To Matt, she said, "Go after him. Tell him I can go home by myself. I'll be good."

"You can't take care of yourself, Elizabeth. You have to stay down."

"But our nurses are overworked as it is. Until we get some more help, it's going to be a madhouse with all these pregnant women and only Dave. I can't—"

"Hush, now. You have to think of yourself and Sarah Beth. Would it be better if you could go somewhere else, let someone else take care of you?"

"Well, yes, but…are you thinking The Way Station? I don't—"

"Nope. I'll be back in a minute." Matt left the room.

"DAVE?" MATT CALLED as he walked into the waiting room. Dave sat behind the receptionist's desk, a phone in his hand.

"Just a minute," he said into the phone. "What is it? Is she okay?"

"She's fine, but she's fretting over causing more work."

"Can't be helped. She has to stay in bed for at least twenty-four hours, maybe longer, if we're going to keep her baby from coming too soon."

"I know. But I can take her to Willie. She'll give her excellent care, and we'll make sure she stays in bed."

Dave looked relieved. "Willie won't mind?"

"Nope, she loves to have a chick to worry over and boss around."

"If you're sure, that would help a lot." Dave spoke into the phone. "I think the problem's solved, Evelyn. Come in at the regular time." He hung up the phone and stood. "Elizabeth agreed?"

"I haven't asked her, but she'll agree. Let me give Willie a call."

A brief conversation with his housekeeper confirmed what he already knew. She was eager to welcome Elizabeth. She also offered to call his family. They'd all become alarmed when he'd gone out in the storm.

He returned to the examining room to discover Dave had already told Elizabeth his plan.

"Matt, I appreciate the offer, but I don't think it's a good idea. Willie has a lot to do. I don't want to cause her more work."

"Willie gave me strict orders to bring you out as soon as the doc okays it. I don't dare go home without you," he told her, grinning.

Tears filled her eyes. "It's…it's so nice of both of you."

"No tears, now. I don't know how to cope with those," he warned her.

She sniffed. "No, no tears. Just gratitude. You've done so much for me."

"Hey," Dave interrupted, clearly trying to lighten the moment, "I forgot to tell you congratulations on your television stardom, Matt. You were quite a hit."

"You saw it?" Elizabeth asked, staring at her comrade.

"Oh, yeah. We watched and recorded it, too. I bet the mail will increase a lot. Good thing you organized those committees."

"Is Sally helping out?"

"Yeah, but I'm going to keep my eye on her. She tries to do too much." He nodded at Elizabeth. "Like a certain doctor I know."

"Isn't that the truth?" Matt said with a sigh.

Elizabeth closed her eyes, ignoring them both.

"It's partly my fault for getting sick," Dave added.

"You couldn't help that," Elizabeth said, not opening her eyes.

"You getting sleepy?" he asked, stepping closer to take her pulse.

"Is it supposed to make her sleepy?" Matt asked, alarm in his voice.

"It can. It relaxes her. At this time of the morning, it wouldn't hurt if she went back to sleep."

"I have to pack a bag," she suddenly said.

"You're not supposed to move around, remember?" Dave said.

Matt jumped in. "I'll go gather a few things for you while you're resting. Where are your keys?"

"You can't pack for me. I...someone—" Her eyes fluttered open and she stared at him.

"Maybe I'll get one of the girls to help me. How's that? Then I'll come back and take you home to Willie. Where are your keys?"

She pointed to her coat, and he dug in the pockets until he found her keys. He held them up for her to see, then pocketed them.

With a nod to the doctor he left the room.

He went straight to her house. He had no intention of getting help from anyone else. In the closet in the baby's room, he found several suitcases. He carried them into Elizabeth's bedroom and began emptying drawers into them.

After he'd completely filled three bags, including her toiletries, he loaded them in the back of the truck. He could come back later if she needed anything else. Hopefully, he'd move the rest of her belongings soon.

He stood one last time in the room he'd helped her prepare for Sarah Beth. It waited for the newborn's arrival. But he renewed his determination. He'd have a few days with Elizabeth, and he was going to do all he could to convince her that she, and Sarah Beth, belonged with him.

After almost losing her yesterday, he wasn't going to give her more time or more distance.

He needed her. And she and Sarah Beth needed him. They all belonged together.

He'd discovered he didn't need someone to cook for him. He had Willie. He didn't need someone to sew things. Or to wait on him. But he needed Elizabeth. He needed her heart, her care, her child...her love.

WHEN ELIZABETH SAW the three large bags in the back of Matt's truck, she frowned. "Why did you pack so much? I'll only be there a day or two. Dave said."

"We'll see. I didn't want you to be missing anything."

Since she was wrapped in his arms, her own arms around his neck, she was close enough to Matt to be able to see his eyes. But she couldn't read the expression there.

"Okay," she finally said. What else could she say? He was doing her a favor, packing for her, taking her home with him, like a lost puppy. She couldn't complain.

"Did you call Willie?"

"You know I did," he said calmly. "I told you she insisted I bring you at once. She's anxious to fuss over you."

As he was sliding her onto the seat, she noticed a big cardboard box in the back of the truck also. "Did you buy a television?"

"Uh-huh." He closed the door and walked around to the driver's side.

"Don't you have a television already?"

"Not upstairs."

She thought about his answer, thinking she was missing something. Her foot knocked against a package on the floorboard. "What's this?"

"Movies." He'd started the truck, and they were already on the way to his ranch.

"Movies?"

"Yeah."

"Why? I thought you said you didn't rent movies."

"Changed my mind."

"Matt, what's going on?" She'd figured it out already, but she wanted to hear it from him.

"Thought maybe it'd give you something to do, some movies to watch. I picked out some of my favorites and some the lady recommended."

"That's so sweet of you," she said, her eyes filling with tears again. She was becoming a regular watering pot. "And you bought the television."

"Hell, Elizabeth, most houses have two or three of them. It's no big deal."

"I'll pay you for—"

"You'll do no such thing," he said sternly. "I'll move it into my room and watch…football. I'll watch football after you're gone. It's my television set."

She stared at him, knowing if he looked at her he'd know how she felt. But she also knew he wouldn't look. He concentrated on his driving, and she got control of her emotions. But his tenderness, his thoughtfulness, meant so much to her.

He was a natural nurturer, doing things for others, taking care of them. Even if he didn't love her, she was fortunate to have his protection.

As predicted, Willie was waiting for them when they arrived. Matt carried Elizabeth to the back door, and Willie held it open.

"Everything all right?" she asked anxiously.

"Doc says she's fine, as long as she keeps off her feet. And you're going to do that, aren't you?" he asked, giving her a hard look.

A hard look that hid a heart made of marshmallow. She was on to Matt McIntyre now. "Of course," she promised solemnly.

"Is her bed ready?"

"Sure is. I put her in the room next to yours, in case she needed something during the night. I couldn't hear her down here," Willie explained.

Pressed against Matt's warm, virile body, Elizabeth tried to suppress the tremors that ran through her when she thought of a bed and Matt at the same time.

Last night had proven it was a dangerous combination.

"You cold?" he quickly asked.

"No, I'm fine."

He carried her up the stairs without even breathing hard.

"I hope we're not too heavy. You're carrying a double-decker, you know." He probably thought a double-decker bus, she guessed with a pang.

"You and Sarah Beth are as light as feathers," he assured her with a smile. He set her on the edge of the bed. "I'm going down to get your bags. You stay put."

Willie came in as he was leaving. "I've got a bed-rest pillow, so you can sit up a little. Is that all right?"

"Yes, Willie, thank you," she said, leaning forward so Willie could put the pillow in place. "I'm sorry to put you to all this trouble."

"It's no trouble. I'll be glad of the company." Willie then eased her shoes off and covered her with a feather comforter. "This'll keep you warm."

"Oh, my, yes."

Matt came in with the three large suitcases.

"My stars, boy, how many bags have you got there?"

His cheeks reddened. "Three. I wanted to be sure we had everything she'll need."

"I think he packed enough for a month, Willie, but I swear Dave said I'd only need to stay in bed for a day or two. You won't be saddled with me forever."

"Yes, she will," Matt contradicted. "I'm not planning on you going back to that house all alone."

Chapter Fifteen

Matt McIntyre was impulsive. He was determined. And he was definitely stubborn.

But he wasn't stupid.

When he saw the panic on Elizabeth's face, he swiftly added, "Until after the baby is born. I don't think you should live by yourself until after Sarah Beth arrives. It's too dangerous."

Elizabeth sank back against the pillows. "I can't stay here that long. I'm not due for another month. That's too much work for— I'll be able to get up after a couple of days."

Willie glared at him and then smoothed out her features to look at Elizabeth. "Of course you will. That's all you need to worry about, honey child. Just relax and rest so you can get back to normal. Now, I've almost got lunch fixed. After I bring up a tray, I'll unpack your things."

"Willie, you're going to get tired climbing the stairs all the time," Elizabeth protested.

"I'm staying in today, so I'll carry things up and down," Matt interjected. After a glance at Willie, he added, "Tomorrow, if everything goes okay, maybe you can spend some time on the couch downstairs.''

Willie gave him a pat of approval as she walked past him. "I'll bring your lunch up in a few minutes.''

Matt stared at Elizabeth when the two of them were left alone. She was lying against the pillows, her eyes closed, her face pale.

He moved closer, then sat down on the edge of the bed. At the sudden movement, her eyes popped open.

"You feeling all right?''

"Yes, fine. I'm just worried about being so much trouble to both of you.''

He had to find a way to relieve her concern, or he'd never get her to stay beyond a day or two. "Look, Elizabeth, out here in the country, we use the barter system a lot. If you're worried about Willie doing too much for you, offer to give her an exam free. I don't think she's been to the doctor in a few years. She's probably due a checkup.''

"Well, of course, I'll be glad to do that. Why hasn't she had a checkup?''

Matt figuratively patted himself on the back. Elizabeth immediately concentrated on Willie's health instead of her own. "Hasn't been sick,'' he told her with a smile.

"But she should have checkups,'' she insisted.

"You're right. I'm greatly relieved that she'll have one now. Thanks, I owe you one.''

His self-congratulations disappeared as Elizabeth's gaze narrowed. "You know good and well you don't owe me, Matt McIntyre. You're just trying to make me feel better!''

With a sigh he took her hand. "Maybe a little, but I didn't say anything that wasn't true."

"About Willie, maybe, but saying you owe me is ridiculous.''

"Think about it, Elizabeth. Remember your refrigerator when I first went to your house? Mine could look the same. Without Willie, everything would fall apart around here. There'd be no food, no clean clothes, no nothing. I'd be spending all my time trying to take care of those things and the ranch work wouldn't get done.''

He lifted her hand to his lips and placed a soft kiss on it. "You take care of Willie, and she takes care of me. So, yeah, I owe you one."

"You're still exaggerating, but I'm glad I can do something for her.''

"Yeah," he agreed with a grin. "Now, I'm going to bring in the television and connect it up. While I'm doing that, you can look at the movies I chose and decide which one you want to watch this afternoon.'' With another kiss to her hand, he stood and left the room.

Time to go downstairs and break the news to Willie that she was going to have a checkup. That fact would make her so happy she might just feed him poison for dinner.

ELIZABETH DIDN'T HAVE TIME to get bored. Not only did Matt connect the television, giving her the chance to watch him work, but she also had several visitors. Annie, Josie and Bailey all came to visit, bringing novels, crossword puzzles and even some quilting pieces.

Bailey had the idea of making a quilt with material from all the pregnant women in town, which would be auctioned off, also. She thought Elizabeth might hem some of the squares.

Elizabeth gave her an incredulous look. "Me? I don't sew."

"It's really basic," Bailey assured her. She demonstrated the slip stitch she wanted her to use. "If you don't feel like it, it's okay."

Sighing, Elizabeth gave her a faint smile. "I suppose I can do a few. In between watching the thousands of movies Matt rented."

"Matt rented movies?" Josie asked in surprise. "He never— There's a television in here!" she suddenly exclaimed.

"Matt bought it this morning. He's being very sweet. I feel bad that he's going to so much trouble."

The other three ladies shared a smile.

Then Annie said, "It's good for him."

"Don't any of you start talking about his taking care of me. It's just that he's such a mother hen. He'd do the same for any of you," Elizabeth protested, realizing what they were thinking.

"You're right," Bailey agreed, still smiling. "He would. Jeff is just as caring. That's one of the things I love about the McIntyre men."

"Yeah," Annie agreed. "When Alex was here, he tried to do everything. I miss him."

"Justin's the same way. That's the neatest thing about marriage," Josie said, her gaze fixed on nothing in particular. "I mean, I do things for him, and he does things for me, and no one keeps count. But you've always got someone around who can be strong when you're weak and vice versa."

Elizabeth closed her eyes. She didn't want the others to see the longing in her gaze. Matt was so caring, so gentle. But his care was on loan. She'd have to go back to being the only strong one, the only adult, in a few days. She couldn't grow too weak by depending on him.

Suddenly the man of her thoughts appeared in the doorway. "Willie wants to know if pregnant ladies would enjoy her chocolate bundt cake with a glass of milk."

There was an immediate approval of that suggestion.

"I'll bring up a tray."

"Wouldn't it be easier if we came downstairs?" Josie asked. Then, at Matt's frown, she remembered. "Oh. Oh, of course, let's have it up here."

"I think we should go down, if Matt wouldn't mind carrying me," Elizabeth said.

"Doctor said—" Matt began.

"Not to walk," Elizabeth finished. "If you're carrying me, I won't be walking. And I won't get bedsores."

"Bedsores?" Matt immediately questioned, his brows coming together.

Elizabeth shot a look at Annie, the only other health professional in the room, even if her subject was animals.

"Elizabeth is right," Annie immediately responded. "Mentally, too, it's good to vary the environment so the patient doesn't lack stimulation."

Matt stood there, his hands on his hips, weighing their words, and Elizabeth thought she'd never seen a sexier man. Then he gave an abrupt nod.

"Okay, you ladies go down and tell Willie. And have her find a stool for Elizabeth to put her feet on." Then he turned to look sternly at her. "Half an hour, young lady. Then you're back up here in bed."

"Yes, Daddy," she told him in mock meekness.

She regretted her words when his cheeks turned red and the other pregnant ladies giggled. They all scurried out before he could issue another reprimand.

Elizabeth apologized as he approached the bed. "I'm sorry, Matt, but you sounded just like my father, laying down the law when I was a little girl."

He cocked one eyebrow at her. "Little girls need someone to lay down the law. They're usually too spoiled if someone doesn't set limits. I can do that for Sarah Beth."

Her heart skipped a beat. "I don't believe you," she finally said, her voice slightly breathless. "I bet she'll have you wrapped around her finger in no time."

He scooped her up, holding her high against his heart. "You could be right," he whispered. "Her mother certainly does."

Then he carried her downstairs.

AFTER HER GUESTS LEFT and Elizabeth returned to her bed, she fell asleep. Matt set the movies aside and stood over the bed, fighting the urge to cuddle her against him.

He had to give her time. But with her so near, he didn't have the patience to wait. Last night he thought they'd had a breakthrough, but today she tensed every time he touched her. With a sigh, he tucked the cover more closely around her and went downstairs.

"How is she?" Willie asked when he entered the kitchen.

"Sound asleep."

"Good. I think bringing her downstairs was a good idea. Won't make her feel so trapped."

"Yeah."

"And you're going to have to watch yourself."

His head snapped up and he stared at his housekeeper. "What are you talking about?"

"You're goin' to scare her off if you don't give her time to get used to the idea."

"What idea?"

"Her bein' your woman. I'm assuming you're plannin' to marry her, though it don't seem like the McIntyre brothers are too keen on the idea." Willie was peeling potatoes for the evening meal, her back to Matt.

"Hey! That's not fair. I'd marry her in a minute," he protested, before realizing what he'd admitted. "I mean—I love her, Willie. I didn't think I ever would love anyone else, but Elizabeth is...is special."

"That she is. I'll do everything I can to help you, too. It'll be great to have a little one around the house. You say she's having a girl? They're the sweetest things.''

''Yeah,'' Matt agreed, smiling.

''And she'll have lots of cousins to play with, if your brothers will take care of business, too.''

''They will. You know Jeff and Bailey are planning on a Christmas wedding while Mom and Dad are here. And Alex will come to his senses. I heard the other day that he's riding that horse of his in the championships in Denver 'round New Year's. I'm betting he'll come home after it's over.''

''I hope Annie will let him come home.''

Matt sat at the table, thinking about the mistake his baby brother was making. Not being there for the birth of his child. He'd like to shake him.

''Yeah,'' he finally said.

''I'm thinking you need to go out and cut down a Christmas tree.''

Matt stared at Willie, startled by the change of subject. ''Now? We always put up the tree after Mom and Dad get here.''

''I know. But the wedding is going to complicate Christmas this year. And it would give Elizabeth something to concentrate on.''

''She can't help with the decorating, Willie. She's not allowed to get up.''

''No, but she could sit on the couch and direct us. She could feel like part of the family, participating in Christmas. It breaks my heart to think of her going back to that house all alone.''

It bothered Matt, too. Willie was right. The more Elizabeth participated in their lives, shared their hours, the easier it would be to convince her to stay. At least, he hoped so.

"Good thinking, Willie. I'll go look for a tree while she's sleeping. Don't let her get up while I'm gone." He hurried into his coat and gloves, grabbed his hat and left the house.

"Lord have mercy, I hope that girl doesn't break his heart," Willie muttered, watching him from the kitchen window.

ELIZABETH WOKE from her nap feeling refreshed. And in need of a trip to the bathroom. She shoved back the covers and slowly stood, taking a moment to get her balance. Then she crossed the room to the hallway.

The bathroom was just across the hall.

She'd washed her hands and was drying them, ready to return to bed, when she heard heavy boots on the stairs. It was ridiculous the way her heart raced at the thought of seeing Matt again. He'd only been out of her sight a couple of hours.

But that thought didn't stop her from opening the door, a smile on her face. Just in time to hear him roar her name.

"Elizabeth?"

He stood staring into her bedroom, his back to her.

"Yes?"

He spun around, almost losing his balance. "What are you doing out of bed?" he thundered.

Before she could answer him, he snatched her into his arms and carried her back to bed.

"I had to go to the bathroom," she said as he lowered her onto the mattress.

His fierce frown didn't fade away at her explanation. "You should've called me."

"Matt, Dave didn't mean I couldn't go to the bathroom. I'm not supposed to be on my feet much, but even in the hospital I'd be allowed to go to the bathroom."

"There's no need while I'm around. I can carry you," he insisted.

She tried to lighten the moment with some humor. "Matt, as many times as I get up during the night, you wouldn't get any sleep at all if I called you every time."

"I've gone without sleep before," he muttered without the slightest hint of a smile.

"You don't expect me to— Matt, I'm not going to get you out of bed during the night," she informed him, exasperation in her voice.

Willie appeared in the doorway. "You two going to argue all night or come to dinner?"

Elizabeth didn't know whether to laugh or cry. It seemed Willie managed to boss Matt around at will, but she, Elizabeth, couldn't even convince him of common sense.

Matt reached over to lift her into his arms. "Put your arms around my neck," he ordered when she didn't move.

She thought about crossing her arms and refusing, but she knew that behavior would be childish. Looping her arms around his neck, she breathed in his scent, feeling again the peace that his presence gave her. Even when he irritated her.

Willie went ahead of them, now that she'd given them orders, and was setting the dishes on the table when they reached the kitchen.

"Arguing isn't good for the baby," she proclaimed, then pulled out her chair and sat down.

Elizabeth stole a look at Matt but said nothing. He ignored both women, as if no argument had ever taken place. After a brief blessing, he passed the dishes of food, then turned his attention to eating.

"Did you watch any movies this afternoon?" Willie asked.

"No. After the girls' visit, I closed my eyes for a few minutes and didn't wake up until just now," Elizabeth told her. "Maybe I'll watch one tonight."

"I might watch it with you," Willie said, "if you don't mind. I haven't watched a movie in years."

"I'd love for you to join me. If…if Matt wanted to watch, too, we could use the television in the living room, so everyone could be comfortable."

He raised his gaze and stared at her. "If you lie down on the couch, we could do that."

She nodded and said nothing else. Willie was right. She needed to avoid arguing with Matt.

"And it will be good practice for tomorrow," Matt added casually as he turned his attention back to his food.

"Tomorrow?"

"Willie suggested we go ahead and decorate the Christmas tree. I thought we could do that after Sunday dinner, while everyone is here. You can lie on the sofa and give directions."

"I wouldn't want to intrude," she said, but excitement filled her at the thought of participating in such a family event. She remembered decorating the tree as a child. Although her parents had been present, there had been no other children. Just her.

"Nonsense," Willie said. "We all join in."

Matt just stared at her.

With a deep breath and a big smile, she said, "I'd like that."

"Good. When we finish, I'll go get the movies from upstairs and we'll vote on which one to watch," Matt said.

Elizabeth decided to tease him, just a little. She wanted him to smile at her. "Don't I get to pick the movie since I'm the sick one?"

He cocked one eyebrow at her. "You're not sick. You're pregnant. We'll vote."

She pretended to pout.

And like the sweet marshmallow she knew he was, he added, "But I reckon I'll like the same movie as you."

SURPRISINGLY, they'd all agreed on a movie, and when it was over, Matt decided they'd made a good choice. Elizabeth had selected *Charade,* an old movie that combined mystery with romance and comedy. He'd enjoyed it.

Elizabeth and Willie had, too. When he'd carried Elizabeth up to her bedroom, she'd been relaxed and smiling, which had been a change from how she'd felt at dinner.

He hadn't intended to upset her, but he'd panicked when he'd gone to her bedroom and found her missing. His heart had double-clutched and then gone racing, as fear had filled him.

He left her in Willie's care in the bathroom across the hall, only after making Willie promise to call him when Elizabeth was ready for bed.

Then he climbed to the attic. The Christmas decorations were stored there, and he wanted to make sure he had everything they needed for tomorrow. The beaming smile on Elizabeth's face when she'd accepted his invitation to help decorate for Christmas had pleased him.

No matter that he'd avoided being present when his parents had put up the tree the past two years. It was time to live again, to celebrate the goodness in life.

Christmas was a great time for that kind of celebration. Especially this year, when the new year, the new millennium, would begin with new life. It didn't matter whose baby was first. They were all a celebration of life.

He picked up a box and started down the stairs. Peeping out of the cardboard was one of his favorite ornaments, one he had forgotten about in his misery. It was a rocking horse.

He'd gotten the ornament when he was six, and each year he hung it on the Christmas tree. It wasn't in pristine condition. One year Alex had chewed on it. Another, Josie had taken it off the tree because she'd wanted to play with it. It had fallen to the floor and broken. But his mother had glued it back together.

Next year he'd show it to Sarah Beth. She'd probably chew on it, too. And he'd get her her own special ornament each year. One that would hold memories of love, so that she'd never forget, wherever she went, that she was part of a family.

But he didn't plan on her going anywhere for the next twenty or so years.

With a smile he took the box to the living room. Time to get ready for tomorrow.

THE HOUSE WAS DARK and silent.

Matt should've been asleep hours ago, but he lay in his bed, intently listening. He was afraid Elizabeth might need him.

Or that she'd refuse to let him know she needed him.

They never had settled their argument this afternoon. So he lay there, unable to sleep as long as he worried about her.

Finally he rolled out of his big bed and padded to the door in his pajama bottoms, worn in honor of their guest. He hadn't closed the door, so he'd be able to hear. Swinging it farther back, he stepped out into the hallway. After Elizabeth had gone to bed, he'd eased her door open, too. He tiptoed to the door and peered in.

He could see the lump in the bed that represented Elizabeth and Sarah Beth. But her posture wasn't relaxed, natural.

"Elizabeth," he whispered.

She raised her head at once. "Yes?"

"Are you all right?"

"Of course."

"Need to make a pit stop?"

"I...I was thinking about it," she whispered.

He crossed to the bed and pulled down the

covers. He'd already seen her long flannel gown. It provided all the modesty she needed. Lifting her into his arms, he carried her to the bath across the hall.

"I'll wait for you here," he told her.

With a nod, she closed the door.

A couple of minutes later, she opened it again.

Scooping her up in his arms, he studied her pale face. "Have you slept at all?"

She shrugged her shoulders but didn't answer.

"Are you worried?"

Reluctantly she nodded. "But I'm feeling fine," she added.

"I haven't slept, either. I miss you." He'd held her close last night and he longed to do so again.

Instead of answering, she tightened her hold around his neck and hid her face against him.

He made an immediate decision. Instead of returning her to her room, he carried her into the master bedroom. When he lowered her to his bed, she opened her eyes.

"This isn't my room."

"It's mine. If you're going to get better, you need your sleep. And I certainly need mine. I think we'll do better together than apart."

"No, Matt!" she protested, panic in her voice.

"Why not? We slept together last night."

"And look what happened! I didn't— You weren't able to—"

"Are you trying to tell me you're going to get me all excited again?" he asked, a big grin on his face.

Her cheeks flamed and she looked away. "Matt, please, I know it's my fault, but I can't—"

"What's your fault?"

"I led you on last night, but I was vulnerable, frightened."

"Do you have that excuse tonight?" He'd worried about her reasons for letting him get close. He'd wanted to believe that she cared about him as he cared about her. But he hadn't been sure.

"No," she whispered.

He scooted her over and slid in after her. "Good." Without waiting for her to say anything, he cuddled her against him, loving the feel of her, the connection he felt to both her and the baby.

"But what about Willie? She'll think—"

"Don't worry about Willie. I'll explain everything."

After a minute she whispered, "I need to sleep on my side."

He helped her shift until they lay spoon fashion. His arm slid beneath her swollen belly to help support the weight. It wasn't long before he heard the soft, even breathing of someone at rest.

He'd have preferred a few kisses before she turned her back on him, but after the fear this morning, he could be content with holding her. Until after the baby was born. With a smile on his face, he fell asleep, too, content now that Elizabeth and Sarah Beth were safe in his arms.

Chapter Sixteen

Willie fixed breakfast at the usual time the next morning. She didn't expect Elizabeth to appear so early, but she figured Matt would follow his normal routine. At least until Elizabeth awakened.

When she didn't hear him moving about, she climbed the stairs. His door was open so she looked in. She almost called his name before she realized what she was seeing.

Cuddled in the bed were Matt and Elizabeth, both of them sound asleep.

Willie hastily backed out of the room, a big grin on her face. She hurried downstairs to put breakfast on hold. Then she called the foreman and told him Matt was unavailable this morning unless they needed him.

After pouring herself another cup of coffee, she sat down to make a list of preparations needed for the noon meal, but all she could think about was Matt with his arms wrapped around the sleeping Elizabeth.

"That boy is faster than I thought. I hope Jeff and Bailey won't mind a double wedding."

MATT AWAKENED FIRST. But he didn't move. Even before he opened his eyes, he smelled Elizabeth's sweet scent, felt her warmth. It had been years since he'd awakened so happy, so content.

So he lay there, holding her, enjoying life.

When she finally stirred, he greeted her with a kiss on her cheek.

"Time for another trip to the bathroom?" he whispered.

"Aren't you sick and tired of carting me around yet?"

"Nope. I'm loving it. I figure once you're not pregnant, I'll have a hard time keeping up with you."

She pulled away slightly, and he prepared himself. He'd been afraid she'd be upset about what had seemed reasonable during the darkness of the night.

He was right.

"We shouldn't have— I should've stayed in my bed last night."

"Why? It worked out pretty well, I think. We both got a good night's sleep."

"Matt! I woke you up a lot. I don't know how many times, but—"

"Doesn't matter how many. I slept in between trips, instead of lying here in the dark worrying. And you slept, too. I bet you feel better this morning."

"I should. All I've done is rest," she returned, sounding grouchy.

"After another day of behaving, Dave will probably let you get up some. So stop fussing."

"Some? I intend to go back to work."

"What? Elizabeth, that's crazy."

"No, it's not. I'm supposed to deliver a lot of babies. It's my job."

"What about your own baby?"

She pushed up on one elbow, staring down at him. "You know I won't do anything to harm Sarah Beth. I'll be careful."

"I know, but…okay, okay, I know you will. But you can't stop me from worrying about you."

To his surprise she lay back down, facing him this time. "I know. And it feels kind of good, actually," she said with a smile.

Her response flooded him with pleasure. Without thinking, he kissed her. Not the casual brush of his lips, as he'd done before, but a lover's kiss, a joining of the soul as well as the flesh. The kind they'd exchanged in the cabin. A kiss that she responded to, initially.

Until she had time to think.

Then she pushed away from him, scooting to the edge of the bed, panic in her eyes.

"Don't fall off!" he warned, reaching for her.

"No! No, I won't, but…don't touch me."

Cautiously he withdrew his hand and sat up. "Whatever you say." He slid off his side of the bed and came around it. "Ready to go to the bathroom?"

As if it dawned on her that a trip to the bathroom meant he'd be touching her again, she tensed, then nodded reluctantly.

He only wished the bathroom was several blocks away, so he could hold her longer. When she emerged, he said, "You want breakfast in bed or in the kitchen?"

"I'm not dressed," she said, but he could read the longing in her face as she looked at the bedroom door. She wanted to escape his room.

"There's no one to see you but me and Willie. Let's go see if she's got breakfast ready." In fact, he figured she'd prepared breakfast hours ago. He couldn't believe he'd slept this late, even with a late night.

While Elizabeth had been in the bathroom, he'd pulled on jeans and a T-shirt, so he, at least, was dressed for breakfast. When they reached the kitchen, Willie was standing at the stove.

"Got anything to feed some hungry cowpokes?" Matt asked with a smile.

"I reckon I can find something. Have a seat."

He appreciated Willie not saying anything about his tardiness. He didn't want Elizabeth thinking she'd caused him any problems.

"I talked to Roy. Everything's fine," she said, naming his foreman.

"Good, thanks."

They chatted about commonplace things during the meal.

Elizabeth had remained silent for a while, but by the time they finished eating, she'd relaxed enough to join in.

Matt figured it was the kiss that had affected her. It certainly had affected him. So much that he wanted to carry her upstairs and repeat it a thousand times. He'd never thought a woman eight months pregnant would turn him on, but Elizabeth did.

Because she was Elizabeth.

After breakfast she said, "Willie, could you spare a few minutes to help me dress?"

"Sure can."

Matt carried her upstairs while Willie followed. He bypassed his room with no comment. Since Elizabeth had started the night in her bed, it looked as if it had been slept in. Willie would never know about last night.

He wasn't sure what he'd do about tonight.

After setting Elizabeth down, he left the two women alone and went downstairs to do their breakfast dishes.

When Willie came down a few minutes later, she thanked him for his help.

"By the way, if Elizabeth's going to sleep in your room, you should move the television in there so she can watch the movies."

He dropped one of the plates on the floor.

ELIZABETH HAD BEEN EXCITED about decorating the Christmas tree with the McIntyre family, but now she was reluctant to come downstairs.

Not that she would have a choice. Matt would appear in her room any minute and carry her down whether she wanted him to or not.

She wished she could believe he'd have put her in his bed whether she'd wanted him to or not, too. But she knew he wouldn't have insisted she sleep with him. Just as she knew she hadn't protested.

But she'd been tired. And scared. Worried about her baby and missing Matt's strong arms. She'd been too weak to think straight in the middle of the night.

So what was her excuse for this morning? She needed an excuse. It was hard to forgive herself for practically seducing Matt this morning. She was eight months pregnant, for heaven's sake! How could she even *have* sexual thoughts right now, much less act on them? But the night in the cabin had told her she did, and she could. It was a wonder Matt hadn't gotten mad and called her a tease. So in reality she had no excuse for letting him put her back in the bed with him.

She knew he cared about her. Dale had cared about her. And she'd cared about him. That mild feeling didn't describe how she felt about Matt. Or how she wanted him to feel about her.

Just her. Not her and Sarah Beth.

How horrible to be jealous of your unborn child.

She wanted Matt to love her, to feel his world revolved around her. To want her. Oh, not now. She knew no man would want someone in her condition. And even if he did, she wasn't about to disrobe in front of him when she looked like a whale. Or maybe the *Titanic* going down.

But one day, when she'd recovered, she hoped Matt could see her as a person, as a woman.

A woman who couldn't cook.

A woman who couldn't sew.

A woman who wouldn't spend her days making a home for him.

She groaned. In her eagerness to be near Matt, to have him touch her, to hope for the future, she'd forgotten her shortcomings.

Damn, damn, damn! "Sorry, baby," she whispered, rubbing her stomach. Even thinking curse words seemed inappropriate around her baby.

Tears filled her eyes and she sniffed, desperately trying to keep them from falling.

"Elizabeth? Are you all right?" Matt asked, hurrying to the bed.

She turned startled eyes to him, and a tear escaped, sliding down her face. She hurriedly wiped it away. "I—I'm fine!"

He scooted her over and sat down on the bed. "Then why are you crying?"

"I'm not. Is everyone here? Is it time to go down?"

"Yeah, they're all clamoring for food. You sure you're all right?"

"Yes, of course."

He stood, then lifted her into his arms. She settled against him, unable to stifle her sigh of contentment. At least for today she could be close to him.

"Elizabeth?" he said again.

She looked up at him. "Yes?"

His mouth descended to hers, and he repeated their morning kiss, his lips teasing hers, then deepening their mating as she opened to him. When he finally raised his head, she had to work hard to keep from pulling his mouth down to hers again.

"We'd better go down," he said.

She nodded, suddenly afraid that she'd look so guilty when they got downstairs, everyone would know she'd spent the night in his arms.

Instead, they were waiting at the table, their interest centered on the food.

WHEN MATT CARRIED HER upstairs for the last time that night, she felt sure she'd go to sleep at once. What a wonderful day.

Everyone had been there except for Alex and their parents. Even Annie's uncle Dex had joined them. Everyone, including Elizabeth, had been treated like family. There had been a lot of talk about Christmas next year, the babies' first Christmas.

The tree looked glorious. After the others had left, she and Matt and Willie had sat in the big room, the lights off. Only the tree lights glittered in the dark room, competing with the fire in the fireplace for attention. They'd talked softly about the day, about Alex's possible return, about the future.

"Tired?" Matt asked, smiling down at her.

"Yes. I won't have any trouble sleeping tonight."

"Did we overdo it?" he asked, frowning.

"No. It's a happy tired."

"Good." Then he carried her into his bedroom.

"Matt, I can't sleep in here tonight. There's no need." Nothing except the need of her heart to be close to Matt.

"Yes, there is."

"What? What reason?"

"I won't be able to sleep without you. You want me to get up in the morning with bags under my eyes?"

"Matt, you're being ridiculous. And if Willie

finds out, we'll both be in trouble.'' Willie was her only hope to stop this madness, because she wanted to be with him too much to come up with reasons on her own.

''Willie already knows,'' he said calmly, putting her down on his bed. ''Stay here. I'll go get your gown.''

She stared after him, stunned, unable to speak.

When he returned, however, she'd marshaled her forces.

''I don't believe you. Willie doesn't know, or she would've said something. I know she wouldn't approve of us sharing a room.''

''Want me to call her up here so you can ask her?''

''No! But she wouldn't approve,'' she insisted.

He chuckled as he reached for the shirttail of her maternity top. ''Lift your arms.''

''You can't undress me!''

''Sweetheart…okay, can you put this on yourself?''

''Of course I can! But you have to go away.''

''I'll take my turn in the bathroom while you undress. Then you can have a turn.''

When he closed the door behind him, she hurriedly struggled into her gown. She considered scurrying to her bedroom next door, but she knew Matt would come after her. And scold her for walking.

What was she to do? He came out, his chest bare, wearing the pajama bottoms he'd had on that morning.

Distracted, she said the first thing that popped

into her head. "I was surprised to find out you wear pajamas."

He laughed. "Usually I don't. But I thought I wouldn't shock you right away."

Her eyes widened, and she hurriedly looked away. "Matt, I have to go back to my room."

He sat down beside her. "Why, Elizabeth? Don't you like sleeping with me?"

Why did he have to ask that question? "Yes," she admitted, her voice low, "but it's not right. I know you want…want to have what your brothers have, but adopting my baby as your own won't— I mean, you'll find the right woman and have your own baby."

"Oh, but I already have."

She almost forgot to breathe. Finally she asked, "Cathy Carter?"

He snorted in derision. "Hardly."

"Is it…is it someone I've met?"

"Oh, yeah."

He said nothing else, and she could've screamed in frustration. "Aren't you going to tell me?"

"I'm not sure she's ready for me to tell anyone."

"Oh, I see. Well, we definitely shouldn't be sharing a bed when you're about to…to marry another woman." She wanted to burst into tears. Her heart was breaking.

"Who said anything about another woman?" he asked gently, one strong arm going around her.

She stared at him. "But you said…"

"I'm talking about you, Elizabeth. You're the one I've found. You're the one for me."

Her heart sang with ecstasy. Until she remembered. "Not me, Matt. It can't be me."

"Is it too soon after your husband's death? I'll wait, Elizabeth, no matter how long it takes."

She almost moaned aloud. Such sweet words. Such impossible words. "I can't change, Matt."

His other hand came to tip her chin, so he could see her face. "Change? Change what?"

Wearily she explained. "I can't change me, Matt. I'm not like Julie. I can't cook, or sew, or…or be a rancher's wife. I'm a doctor. I have to help my patients. That means long hours and taking care of others, instead of taking care of you. I can't make you happy."

"Really?" he asked in a conversational voice, as if she'd just told him it would be cold tomorrow. "Do you know what's necessary to be a rancher's wife?"

"Of course I do! I just told you—"

He laid a finger over her lips, stopping her. "All that's required to be a rancher's wife is a rancher. And I'm volunteering."

Before she could protest again, he laid her back against the pillows and covered her lips with his. She couldn't keep her arms from going around his neck, from holding him close. She couldn't stop her mouth from opening to his, from worshiping him with all the feelings in her heart.

As his mouth joined hers, his hands stroked and petted her, as he had done in the cabin. She again was able to touch in return, to feel his hard muscles, his sensitive spots. He sloped his mouth over hers again and again, until she couldn't tell where she stopped and he began.

When he slid her gown up her body, she protested. "No, I don't want you to see—"

"See what? See how beautiful you are? How well you're taking care of your baby? Come on, Elizabeth," he whispered before trailing kisses down her neck.

"I'm so big, Matt. You can't want—"

"Honey, I want with every ounce of me!" he exclaimed, his lips reinforcing his words. "I know we need to wait to make love. But there's no reason for me not to kiss you all over, to touch you, for you to touch me."

Such sweet words stopped her protests, but she hid her head against his neck as he pulled her gown from her. His hands caressed her skin, sending tingles through her that brought her own hands to his body. He was such a handsome man, inside and out.

She loved the feel of him, his muscular strength that reminded her of his care of her and her baby. And the laugh lines on his face. Kissing each of them tenderly, she returned to his lips as he lifted his face to hers.

She was swept away by the sensations he evoked, taking her from the realities of life, letting her dreams take over. Letting her forget the doubts that filled her about the future.

Sarah Beth, however, reminded her. She made a staccato protest against her mother's stomach.

Matt's mouth left Elizabeth's, and he reached out to rub Sarah Beth's foot. At least Elizabeth thought it was her foot.

"Hey, little girl, are you afraid we forgot you?" he asked softly. He bent down to place a kiss on Elizabeth's stomach.

Without his kisses, doubt crept back into Elizabeth's head. Her hands fluttered on his broad chest. "Matt? Are you sure? Are you sure I'm not a substitute for what you lost? I love you so much—"

He kissed her again. Then he held her by the shoulders and looked sternly into her eyes.

"Elizabeth Lee, I love you with all my heart. I'll still love you when you're old and gray. I'll love our children, every one of them, starting with this one," he said, putting a hand on her stomach. "I loved Julie, but she's gone. I never thought I could love again, but you stole my heart right away. I wasn't willing to admit it. Not at first. But you gave me no choice."

She reached out to caress his lean cheek. "I…I love you. I just want you to be sure."

"Did you know Willie and Julie didn't always get along?" he asked.

The change of subject puzzled her. "No, I didn't know that."

"You know why?"

She shook her head no.

"They both wanted to be in charge of the kitchen." With a triumphant grin, he said, "We won't have that problem!"

"Matt, be serious," she protested.

"Oh, I'm serious. Wait until Mom gets here. I'm hoping this year she'll be too busy with the wedding and all the prospective grandchildren. Otherwise, you'll see exactly what I mean. After all, the kitchen—Willie's kitchen—was once hers.''

''Oh.''

''Yeah. Julie loved to do those things, so she did them. You love to be a doctor. A good doctor that the community loves. All I care about is that you're happy. And you love me.''

She was starting to believe him, and the glimpse of happiness was incredible. ''I might learn to cook a little,'' she said, hope in her voice. ''In case Willie gets sick.''

''Whatever. You might be better off keeping Willie well. She makes an incredible pot roast.'' But the grin on his face told her he was teasing.

''Oh, Matt, I love you so much!''

''That's all I need, sweetheart, your love. We'll buy our cherry pies from Nell and leave the kitchen to Willie. And live happily ever after.''

Elizabeth could only agree.

Epilogue

Matt sat on the sofa, Elizabeth resting against him, his arm around her. Since she'd moved to the ranch, his life had centered on her and her unborn baby. And he'd never been happier.

"Hear those two in the kitchen?" he whispered in Elizabeth's ear. His mother and Willie were debating menus for New Year's Eve. The entire family intended to gather at the ranch, assuming none of them were in the hospital. After all, the babies were due anytime.

The phone rang, and Elizabeth tensed.

"Don't worry, it's probably a neighbor," he told her, reaching for the phone beside him. Jeff's voice told him differently.

"Matt, is Elizabeth there?" The urgency in his brother's voice alerted Matt. He handed the phone to Elizabeth without comment.

Their conversation was brief, ending with Elizabeth's promise to meet them at the hospital. Matt stood and offered her assistance.

"Why don't you call Dave? It's already late."

He knew the answer before he made his suggestion, but he had to try.

She grinned at him. "Nice try. Bailey is my patient. I'm going."

"Then I'm going, too."

"Good."

Matt's heart swelled with love. Elizabeth never protested his care these days. She hadn't married him yet, because she'd asked that they wait until after Sarah Beth arrived, but she never denied his right to take care of her.

"What do you need from upstairs?" he asked. "I'll run up and get them."

"My shoes. My bag is down here, and my coat. That should be everything. While you're doing that, I'll inform the two in the kitchen. It'll give them something else to argue about."

Her smile reassured him. She'd pleased Willie by staying out of the way, leaving the house to Willie's care. Since his mother's arrival, however, the two ladies had battled.

When he reached the kitchen, Elizabeth was sitting at the table, with the two older women hovering around her.

He knelt and slipped her shoes on her feet, then reached for her arms to help her up.

His mother stopped him. "I don't think Elizabeth should go."

Matt smiled. His parents had taken to Elizabeth big-time. He leaned over and kissed his mother's cheek. "Thanks for worrying, Mom, but Elizabeth knows what she's doing."

Elizabeth sent him a grateful look. "Besides," she added, "your first grandbaby is a big event."

"Should we come now?" his mother asked.

"No. Matt will call you after we get there. First babies can take quite a while to arrive," Elizabeth assured her. Then with a hug for each lady, she hurried to the door, Matt following her.

Once they got to the hospital, Matt stood back out of the way. Jeff and Bailey arrived, and Elizabeth, with one of the nurses to help her, began her examination.

"I'm so nervous," Jeff confessed, sitting with Matt in the reception room. "How long do you think it will take?"

"Elizabeth says it can be a long time." Silence reigned as each man thought about the next few hours.

When the outside door burst open, however, they both leaped to their feet. Annie and Alex, their faces red from the cold, walked in.

Matt and Jeff stared at their youngest brother. Then they both gave him a hug, slapping him on his back.

"What are you doing here?" Matt demanded. "I thought you were riding in Denver."

"Yeah, we were looking for you to come back next week," Jeff added.

"I was afraid Annie would have the baby without me," Alex confessed. Then he squared his shoulders and looked at Matt. "I dropped out of the competition, even though I was leading. Annie and my baby are more important."

Matt's lips curved up in a warm smile. "I couldn't agree more."

Alex stared at his brother, as if he couldn't believe what he'd said. "You do?"

"Yeah, I do."

The significance of their conversation, their appearance, struck Jeff first, aided by Annie clearing her throat. All three men shifted their attention to her.

"Are you all right?" Jeff asked. "I mean, are you in labor?"

As Annie nodded, Alex added, "I got home just in time. We were going to be married, but Sam here wouldn't wait."

"Sam?" Matt asked, his gaze snapping to Alex. "You've named your baby Sam?"

Alex and Annie exchanged a look, but Alex answered, "I hope you don't mind, but Annie wanted—"

"Nope. I don't mind. I think it's great."

Alex stared at his brother, but Annie's gasp drew everyone's attention.

"We can talk later," Matt said. "Let me go tell Elizabeth you're here."

Alex scooped Annie up in his arms and followed him.

MATT CONVINCED ELIZABETH to go back to the ranch with him about two in the morning. The nurse promised to call her if there was any change in Bailey or Annie.

With Elizabeth wrapped in his arms, they grabbed a few hours of sleep. The alarm went off at seven. "How you feeling?" he asked, after kissing her good-morning.

"Fine. I'm calling the hospital."

It was just as well that he knew Elizabeth loved him, because when she had a patient who needed her, she forgot everything around her.

Willie had breakfast ready for them.

"What would I do without you, Willie?" Elizabeth said with a smile.

"We don't intend to find out," Matt said, winking at Willie. "I'm going to go warm up the truck."

"Matt, you don't have to spend the day at the hospital," Elizabeth said, stopping him.

"Yes, I do. Besides, it'll give Dad something to do, filling in for me here." Then he hurried outside. Fifteen minutes later Elizabeth took her first look at her patients. Both McIntyres had spent the night at the hospital with their ladies. Matt pried them away for a quick visit to the café for breakfast, once Elizabeth assured them there was no rush.

In the middle of the afternoon Josie and Justin joined the others at the hospital.

"You, too?" Elizabeth asked, a wide smile on her face. "Still trying to win the contest?"

"Hey, it's New Year's Eve," Josie pointed out.

Matt called his parents a few hours later. "Willie, you and Mom and Dad had better come on. Looks like it won't be long now."

He hurried back to the small office the doctors used, to discover Elizabeth sitting behind the desk. "Mom and Dad and Willie are on their way. They want to greet their new grandbabies."

"Good."

She didn't move, and Matt got a funny feeling in his stomach. "You okay?"

Elizabeth gave him a faint smile. "As okay as I can be, since I'm in labor."

"No! It's still too early! Can Dave give you another shot?"

She shook her head. He put his arms around her, helping her out of the chair.

"Then we'd better get you in a bed," Matt said, hoping she wouldn't notice how fast his heart was beating. With a shout for Dave as he left the office, he picked up Elizabeth and headed for the nearest bed.

Shortly after eleven, Annie gave birth to Samuel McIntyre, with Alex at her side. Willie carried the news to the other family members, moving between the various rooms.

"Is Annie all right?" Elizabeth asked anxiously.

"She's just fine, and glad it's over," Willie reported with a big smile. "And that little boy looks just like his daddy."

Matt squeezed Elizabeth's hand. "Guess there's no doubt who the daddy is now."

"Nope. And Josie's gettin' real close."

A scream interrupted their conversation, and Willie hurried out, only to return five minutes later. "Josie had her little girl. Everyone's fine. Rachel Holcomb gave birth, too. Looks like you and Bailey are the only ones still in the race for the Millennium Baby Contest."

Elizabeth smiled, but another pain gripped her and the smile disappeared. After panting her way through it, with Matt holding her hand, she gasped, "I don't care about the stupid contest."

"Bailey said the same thing," Willie assured her.

Matt hadn't even considered that Sarah Beth might be the millennium baby. He didn't want all that attention. He wanted Elizabeth and Sarah Beth all to himself. But he would even accept winning the contest if it meant lessening the pain Elizabeth was suffering. "Hang in there, sweetheart," he whispered in her ear.

"Matt, go get Dave."

He started to question her, but the urgency on her face stopped him. He rushed from the room.

Ten minutes later, as the clock struck midnight and the sound of fireworks going off filled the room, Dave urged Elizabeth to give one last big push.

Sarah Beth Lee, soon to be McIntyre, entered the world. Elizabeth, tears in her eyes, asked, "Is she all right?"

Dave grinned, assuring her her baby was perfect.

Matt took the baby, wrapped in a blanket by the nurse, to show her to Elizabeth. "Welcome home, Sarah Beth," he whispered as he handed her to Elizabeth.

Dave, however, got everyone's attention as he called out, "Time of birth, 12:01. We have a winner!"

A WEEK LATER, the last of the McIntyre bachelors were married. Both of them. Alex and Annie welcomed Matt and Elizabeth in joining their wedding plans.

Matt and Elizabeth had told Willie and his parents, but the rest of the family had been kept in the dark. After the celebration of the babies, they began celebrating all over again.

One more surprise awaited Matt McIntyre.

To the joy of his new wife and baby girl, he added the prize of Mr. January. Josie had forced him to buy a few chances to be pictured with the winning baby.

When the calendar came hot off the press a couple of days later, there he stood, holding Sarah Beth, a proud smile on his face.

The millennium baby of Bison City, Wyoming, was his. As was her mother. He had his family at last.

The new millennium couldn't have a better start in his opinion.

**Starting December 1999,
a brand-new series about
fatherhood from**

Three charming stories
about dads and kids...
and the women who
make their families
complete!

Available December 1999
FAMILY TO BE (#805)
by Linda Cajio

Available January 2000
A PREGNANCY AND A PROPOSAL (#809)
by Mindy Neff

Available February 2000
FOUR REASONS FOR FATHERHOOD (#813)
by Muriel Jensen

Available at your favorite retail outlet.

HEART OF THE WEST

Every Man Has His Price!

Lost Springs Ranch was
famous for turning young
mavericks into good men.
So word that the ranch was
in financial trouble sent
a herd of loyal bachelors
stampeding back to
Wyoming to put themselves
on the auction block!

July 1999	*Husband for Hire* Susan Wiggs	January 2000	*The Rancher and the Rich Girl* Heather MacAllister
August	*Courting Callie* Lynn Erickson	February	*Shane's Last Stand* Ruth Jean Dale
September	*Bachelor Father* Vicki Lewis Thompson	March	*A Baby by Chance* Cathy Gillen Thacker
October	*His Bodyguard* Muriel Jensen	April	*The Perfect Solution* Day Leclaire
November	*It Takes a Cowboy* Gina Wilkins	May	*Rent-a-Dad* Judy Christenberry
December	*Hitched by Christmas* Jule McBride	June	*Best Man in Wyoming* Margot Dalton

HARLEQUIN®
Makes any time special ™

Visit us at www.romance.net

PHHOWGEN

HARLEQUIN®
AMERICAN ◆ ROMANCE®

Coming in January 2000—
a very special 2-in-1 story...

Two sexy heroes, two determined heroines,
two full romances...one complete novel!

Sophie's a stay-at-home mom.
Carla's a no-nonsense businesswoman.
Neither suspects that trading places for a week
will change their lives forever....

HIS, HERS AND THEIRS (#808)
by Debbi Rawlins
January 2000

Join us for twice the fun, twice the romance
when two sisters-in-law trade places and fall in
love with men they wouldn't otherwise have met!
Only from Harlequin American Romance®!

Available at your favorite retail outlet.

HARLEQUIN®
Makes any time special ™

Come escape with Harlequin's new

Series Sampler

Four great full-length Harlequin novels bound together in one fabulous volume and at an unbelievable price.

Be transported back in time with a Harlequin Historical® novel, get caught up in a mystery with Intrigue®, be tempted by a hot, sizzling romance with Harlequin Temptation®, or just enjoy a down-home all-American read with American Romance®.

You won't be able to put this collection down!

On sale February 2000 at your favorite retail outlet.

HARLEQUIN®
Makes any time special ™